FORGOTTEN
DESTINY

**Center Point
Large Print**

**This Large Print Book carries the
Seal of Approval of N.A.V.H.**

FORGOTTEN DESTINY

A Western Trio

Peter Dawson

CENTER POINT PUBLISHING
THORNDIKE, MAINE

This Center Point Large Print edition
is published in the year 2007 by arrangement with
Golden West Literary Agency.

The text of this Large Print edition is unabridged. In other
aspects, this book may vary from the original edition.
Printed in the United States of America.
Set in 16-point Times New Roman type.

ISBN-10: 1-60285-057-7
ISBN-13: 978-1-60285-057-6

Library of Congress Cataloging-in-Publication Data

Dawson, Peter, 1907-1957.
    Forgotten destiny : a western trio / Peter Dawson.--Center Point large print ed.
        p. cm.
    ISBN-13: 978-1-60285-057-6 (lib. bdg. : alk. paper)
    1. Large type books. I. Title.

PS3507.A848F67 2007
813'.54--dc22

2007017608

TABLE OF CONTENTS

Brand of Luck

Jonathan Glidden, who wrote as Peter Dawson, completed this story in October, 1940. It was sold to *Complete Western Book Magazine* on November 3, 1940. Glidden's title for the story was "An Outcast Deputy's Brand of Luck," and he was paid $108.00 for it. The editor changed the title to "Land-Grabber, I'll Be Back With Guns" for publication in *Complete Western Book Magazine* (3/41). The story was reprinted more than a decade later in *Complete Western Book Magazine* (9/54) as "I'll Be Back, Landhog!" For the story's first book appearance the author's original title has been somewhat shortened.

I

The cabin had lost its air of disuse. New yellow pine shakes unevenly splotched the gray, tinder-dry slant of its roof, and along its sides showed an occasional fresh slab with the bark still brown and yellow. The wagon shed out back gave evidence of the same neat hand, while the lean-to near the corral was new and staunchly built. The green carpet of the valley climbed the knoll and made a pleasing yard out front, a yard now orderly where three months ago brush and rusty tin cans had completed the lay-out's desolate appearance.

Hugh Conner, his tall, flat frame propped indolently

against one corner of his cabin, gazed unsmilingly at the two men standing near their ground-haltered ponies thirty feet out in the yard, and said tonelessly: "No one wanted it, so I'm here."

"Someone wants it now," the tallest of the pair growled, his belligerence obvious. He was thin almost to gauntness, and on the upper left-hand pocket of the vest beneath his canvas windbreaker showed a sheriff's five-pointed star. His light-colored blue eyes were red-rimmed and dull from too much whisky. Sheriff Mace Dow didn't command the respect due his badge.

"Who wants it?"

"I've already filed on it," answered Mace Dow's companion. "One of my crew will be up here next week. He's homesteading in my name."

"Why didn't you come to me before you filed, Keyes?"

Wyatt Keyes lifted his thick shoulders in a careless shrug. "You're a squatter, Conner. I didn't think it necessary to consult you."

His sarcasm was biting, eloquent of the man's habitual arrogance. Looking at Keyes now, Hugh Conner wondered at the stubborn will that had brought the man so far in ten years. This last summer Keyes's Key-Bar had calmly bluffed George Baird's Chain Link, the biggest outfit in this country, and made Baird give over ten sections of choice summer graze high in the hills. A legal loophole had made it possible, and with the help of his sheriff—Mace Dow

8

had two years ago been Key-Bar foreman—he'd made it stick. Now he was buying up this valley. Hugh hadn't been surprised at their call this afternoon, for he had heard of Keyes's visits to some of his neighbors above, but it galled him to have to give up something he had made from nothing and with his own hands. Every day for three months, since the time he had first came to this country, he had worked at his cabin and his fence, believing that it was his home.

"And if I don't get out?"

Keyes and Dow both smiled. "We'll change your mind." As Keyes spoke, he hooked his thumbs significantly in his shell belts within finger spread of the ivory-handled guns slung low in tooled holsters at his thighs. He was full of confidence, his solid body mirroring a physical strength that backed a strong will.

Hugh Conner got the second hint of the reason for their visit from Mace Dow. The lawman's eyes had clouded over, and now the fingers of his right hand clawed and stiffened. So they were here to shoot it out with him!

As his eyes settled on Mace's wrist, knowing that the first sign of the man's draw would be telegraphed plainly, Hugh drawled: "There's an election in town today. Maybe that'll change things."

"Mace will be reëlected sheriff," Keyes answered.

Hugh shook his head. "I reckon not. There are too many decent people in this country to see that happen again."

He saw Mace's wrist muscles bulge, saw that hand

move a fraction of an inch. Suddenly, from far out across the pasture, came the strident, wild yelping of a dog. He saw Mace's hand relax as then both the lawman and Keyes looked out across the valley. His glance followed theirs. A dog was bounding in long strides toward the cabin with a full-grown jack rabbit streaking ahead in twenty-foot leaps. The dog's ears were pointed, and his full-throated cry was piercing and high-pitched, showing a wild ancestry.

As Dow and Keyes looked back at Hugh again, too wary to witness the finish of that race, Hugh saw the dog swing close, not fifty yards away. "Excuse me, gents," he said, shoving himself out from the wall of the cabin. "There's the calf-killer I've been huntin'."

Before they could read his intention, his two hands flowed smoothly up from his sides. They moved faster than the eye could follow, and, when they settled at his hips, they rocked into position two Colt .38s. His right-hand gun bucked in his hand, to send a hollow blast ripping out across the valley; then, in one pro-longed inferno of sound, five more shots beat out. At the first explosion the dog's steady strike broke and his front legs went limp and he rolled over in a sprawl; five times that furry body jerked from a slug's impact. When sudden silence edged out the far echoes of those shots, Hugh slid his weapons back into leather and said: "Now what were you sayin', Keyes?"

Wyatt Keyes's eyes mirrored unfeigned surprise, while Mace Dow's mouth gaped open in sheer astonishment at the gun magic he had witnessed.

Finally Keyes growled: "We'll be back, Conner." He turned. "Let's be goin' Mace." He led the way back to the horses.

Keyes was satisfied with the implications behind his last threat, but Mace Dow wasn't. He reined his pony close in to Hugh and bent down in the saddle to take a parting jibe. "Maybe I ought to look through some of the Reward posters I've been throwin' in that empty drawer of my desk, Conner."

"Maybe you had, Mace. Maybe you'd find your own picture on one of 'em."

Dow's face clouded to a brick red as he swung away, wordless. He had seen enough during the past few minutes to make him ride check on his temper.

When they were out of sight in the bend on the trail below, Hugh signed gustily, took off his Stetson, and wiped the sweat out of its band. It had been too close, much too close, and he was momentarily thankful that these two hadn't driven him to using his guns on them. *I wonder what he knows?* he mused, recalling that last remark of the lawman's. But then his concern left him. Mace Dow couldn't know, or he'd have come up here with a warrant. Four months ago Hugh Conner had spent two nights and three days outriding a posse far to the north. A glory hunter had prodded him into using his guns, and a forked sheriff, fearing the influence of the dead man's friends, had turned a deaf ear to Hugh's plea of self-defense. So there had been a jail break, a deputy with a broken jaw—and that hard ride across the state line.

Now, having found this small, unwanted place and taken it for his own, he was being driven out for no reason that he knew. He would have to go; that much was certain, for Keyes wouldn't be back without guns to back him the next time. Perhaps he wouldn't even bother to come back. There were a hundred places in the timber above the cabin where a bushwhacker could hide to put a bullet between Hugh's shoulders some morning.

He looked out at the dead dog, lying at the border of the pasture. "Thanks, friend," he muttered. "You made up for all the critters you've dragged down in comin' along when you did."

He stood there a moment, wondering what would happen if he stayed and fought Keyes. Mace Dow might lose the election today—although that was unlikely, with all Keyes's backing—and a new lawman might recognize his prior rights to the property. But in staying to fight, he was running a risk. Someone might be curious about him and do what Dow had threatened—look at the Reward dodgers. And there might be one with his name on it.

No, he'd get out of the country, bury himself in obscurity somewhere south, closer to the border. But before he left, he'd make a play that Keyes and Dow wouldn't forget. He already knew how he was going to do it. It would be a petty, unsatisfying revenge, but he wasn't going to crawl out like a whipped dog.

He went out to the lean-to, intent on the first thing to be done. Out there he drained half a bucket of coal oil from a nearly empty barrel and took it to the house. He rolled his few personal belongings into a blanket, and then sloshed the coal oil liberally over his bunk and along the base of the walls. With one last, regretful look at what had been his home for three months, he flicked alight a match and tossed it onto the bunk. A puff of blaze burst outward and climbed the wall, spreading fast.

He fired the lean-to and the wagon shed in the same manner. Ten minutes later, from his saddle on a higher knoll a hundred yards above, he looked down on the lay-out. Three black pillars of smoke plumed high in the still, crisp air, the flames already showing along the cabin's near wall. It would do.

He wheeled his claybank gelding and rode straight up the valley, toward the low pass to the north that cut between the jagged snow-capped peaks ahead. He'd wait out the rest of the day in the timber above, and tonight, late, he'd ride into Bull Forks and hunt up Dow and Keyes and name them as the men who fired his place. The election-crowd would be there, and not many would soon forget his visit.

He was striking into the trees a mile above when his forward glance made out the figure of a rider half hidden beneath the leafless aspens on the trail ahead. Instinctively his right hand fell to his side in a wary gesture, but the next instant he had recognized the rider, and his hand came away.

Fay Baird sat her dun pony with a straight-backed, easy grace that always stirred him to admiration.

Today she was outfitted in worn, blue Levi's, a cotton shirt open at the throat, and a dark brown buckskin jacket that gave only a hint of her squarish shoulders and boyish body. Her hair caught the tree-branched pattern of sunlight and took on a coppery sheen he had never before noticed.

As he drew rein twenty feet away, she frowned in mock severity and said: "Aren't you going to speak to me, Hugh?"

Once again he caught the strong flavor of her friendliness, and he knew that his one regret in leaving this country would be at losing the promise of these rare moments with her. The Chain Link, her home, was ten miles out from this valley, yet he saw her occasionally in town, and, after their first meeting she had been this way, friendly without forwardness, and feeling a measure of the same thing that had attracted him to her.

"You saw me . . . what I did down there?" he queried, wanting to get this over with.

"I did, Hugh. And I saw Keyes and his understrapper ride away. What does it mean?"

"It's Keyes's place now. I'm leavin' as little of it as I can."

"His place? Then he's seen you, too. Dad and a few others are wondering why he wants this valley. Are you leaving, Hugh?"

He nodded his answer.

"Without a fight?" Her look turned abruptly serious. "Without a fight, Hugh?"

"It would be one man against his whole outfit . . .

14

and against his lawman. It's not worth a dose of lead poison for me to stay and find out why he wants this place. I'm pullin' out."

"But it won't be one man against Keyes. Walt Andrews may win the election today. If he does, things will change."

"He won't win. He can't. But suppose he does? That'll be two against Keyes. Not enough."

"But there's Dad. . . ."

"George Baird fight?" Hugh's sudden laughter was mocking. "I don't think so. Your father lost his chance at Keyes when he pulled off that hill range this summer."

"But I intend to make him fight!" Suddenly the flashing in her brown eyes quieted before a resigned look. She sighed, and lifted her shoulders in a shrug. "Of course, Walt Andrews won't win. I came up here to get these people to go down and vote for him. But it won't help much."

To see her high spirits so weighed down by a lost hope made Hugh Conner wish there was some way he could help her and her friends before he left. He stared unseeingly back at the burning cabin, idly turning over in his mind a thought that had just come to him. Abruptly he turned to face the girl. "There's a way you can win that election, Fay." His gray eyes were narrow-lidded now, and a faint smile played across his aquiline features. "How long will it take you to ride to town?"

"An hour if I hurry."

"Four o'clock. That may be time enough." He lifted a hand and pointed to the billowing smoke cloud spreading out above the tops of the trees. "Can you ride in and tell your father and Walt Andrews that you found my place had been fired? Can you put that story across?"

"But it wouldn't be the truth." The shrewd light that had come to her eyes belied the protest.

"It would. You saw Keyes and Dow. Later, you saw my place on fire. You can leave out the rest. Ten minutes after you get that story started, Mace Dow won't get one vote out of ten. It's a way of winning for Walt Andrews. Will you do it?"

She looked at him with a softness in her glance that was a mute plea. "Will you stay, Hugh?"

"What does that have to do with this other?"

"It means you'll be with us fighting Keyes."

"I'll decide that later," he told her. "Right now, you've got a job on your hands. Play it right and you'll win. I'll be in town tonight to see how the election turns out."

He leaned across and slapped her dun across the hindquarters to startle the animal into a quick run. As she headed out across the pasture, she turned in the saddle and waved and called back something he didn't catch.

He sat there watching her, once more feeling that deep regret in losing this friend. He felt better about leaving now; his petty revenge rankled less against his pride, for as it had turned out he was helping the

16

people he would have wanted to help if he stayed. Maybe he could do one more thing to help them before he rode away.

II

Room 14 in the Mountain View Hotel had served as Mace Dow's headquarters throughout the day. Four hours ago it had been full to overflowing with a riotous, odorous crowd of drunken voters. Wyatt Keyes's friend, Faro Mike, owner of the Palace Bar, had loaned his best barkeep for the occasion and supplied all the whisky. Faro Mike expected favors in return, namely, that Dow would continue to let him run his place wide open and to keep on using the itinerant faro and poker dealers who ran the crooked tables in his place. The town ordinance requiring saloons to close at midnight, and restricting the play at gaming tables, had not been enforced for two years. It was to Faro Mike's advantage to see that it wasn't for another two.

The afternoon didn't turn out the way Keyes and Dow and Faro Mike had planned it. Around four o'clock they heard the story that was making the rounds—the story that Hugh Conner had been burned out and that they were being blamed for it. Fay Baird, whose word was gospel, had seen Keyes and his sheriff riding away from Hugh's and had gone on to find his buildings a blazing ruin.

The news had worked like magic. Room 14 had

emptied fast, leaving nothing but a litter of empty bottles and broken glasses, cigarette butts and cigar ash strewn about the floor, and a few drunks asleep in the room's half dozen chairs. Five o'clock had seen Mace Dow's headquarters deserted, and from then on people who hadn't yet voted made no bones about saying which way their ballots were being cast. Walt Andrews was their man, and to hell with Keyes and his crowd!

Now, at nine o'clock, three men waited in Room 14. Across the street was the unused hall above the saddle shop where the election judges were counting the votes, and below in the street waited an eager, boisterous crowd. Mace Dow sat with his ungainly frame slumped in a deep leather chair, his eyes bleary from too much whisky, his speech thick as he muttered: "Half a dozen gents could go across and get those ballots. Burn 'em. And if they called a new election, we'd make sure this time."

Keyes sat with one leg thrown over the corner of a rickety table. He surveyed his lawman with a cold, disgusted stare. "We don't do things that way from now on, Mace. There's plenty of time." He shifted his glance from Dow to the third occupant of the room, a tallish man outfitted in a tight-fitting serge suit and a derby hat who paced restlessly back and forth in front of the window, where a drawn blind cut off the view of the street, and the closed window muffled the mutterings of the crowd below.

"Nothing to worry about, Summers," Keyes said

softly, an easy smile playing across his square features. "The way the election goes doesn't have anything to do with our proposition. You might as well go to your room and turn in."

The stranger, Summers, shook his head emphatically and met Keyes's smile with a quality of stoniness in his eyes that baffled any attempt at heartiness. "I don't like it," he snapped, and it was plain that he was a willful man. "I don't like the smell of the whole thing."

"Maybe you'd like to pull out of the deal."

"Don't be a damn' fool!" Summers blazed, unimpressed. "I've bought myself into this, and I'll play the hand out. But I hate to see a perfect lay-out blasted by a childish move. Why did you do it?"

"Once again, we didn't burn Conner's place," Keyes breathed, his mouth a thin, tight line at his sudden rise of temper. "I tell you it's a frame-up."

"It'll make it harder. You'll have a tough job doing this in three weeks. That's when Sierra Central expects my report on the right-of-way, and I'd better show up with the deeds to all that valley property."

"Since when does a railroad have to settle a matter of right-of-way in three weeks?"

Summers hid his impatience behind a cloak of suavity, his belligerence abruptly giving way before a studied, biting sarcasm. "Once again, Keyes, here are the reasons. Fifty miles west there's another low pass through these hills. We took out an option on the land down there before we knew about this. That option expires in three weeks. The Denver and Southern are ready to take up that option if we release it. They'll build through there. Now! If we can buy up this valley of yours and lay steel through the pass above, well and good. It's better than the other, and means we'll get through ahead of the Denver and Southern. But if we don't get this valley inside of three weeks, we've got to take the other, whether we like it or not. And you're out!"

"And *you're* out!"

"And I'm out. But get this, Keyes. Before I'm out, I'll go to those valley ranchers myself and offer them the full amount, two hundred a section. My future depends on keeping my job with Sierra Central."

"Your future depends on me," Keyes corrected.

For a long, tense moment the two men eyed each other with unveiled hostility. Finally Summers shrugged, smiled, and said: "What the hell are we rowin' about? This will go through, like you say. You've taken out options on most of the valley and bought out a few outfits at twenty and thirty a section. The deal still holds, Keyes. You get a hundred a section for the whole works. I take my cut of fifty and turn back fifty to the railroad. They'll make me a director for saving them the money."

"I wonder," Keyes mused brutally. "I wonder if you'll turn that fifty back to Sierra Central."

"That's something you'll never know, Keyes. And, in case you get any wild ideas, there's a signed and sealed statement in my office safe that'll take care of you if anything happens to me."

"Forget it," Keyes said, trying to smooth over his tone but making a poor effort. "Why would I cut the bottom out of my own pocketbook?"

"Why would you cut your own throat, you mean. Together, we can go a long way. But if you. . . ."

He bit off his words, all at once listening to the undertones of the crowd outside lift to a pulsing roar. Keyes came down off the table, crossed the room to turn down the lamp on the ornamental fireplace, and then went to the window. Mace got up out of his chair and followed, leaning heavily against Summers as the shade went up and Keyes raised the window.

A blast of sound filled the room. The street below was packed with shouting people whose faces were upturned to where a man stood at a lighted window of the room above the saddle shop. Keyes and his companions could see into the room across there, could see the litter of paper that strewed the floor under the long table where the judges had been counting the ballots.

The shouting below died slowly. A few jeers of "Down with Dow!" and "Get rid of Keyes's understrappers!" rang out, and then there was quiet, a silence that flowed out in waves along the half-lighted street to the crowds in front of the saloons. The election judge in the window across the street cleared his throat, and the sound plainly shuttled across the interval to Keyes and his companion. Then came the words: "Ladies and gentlemen. The count has been totaled and certified by the Committee on Elections.

21

For Mace Dow, eight hundred and twenty-two votes. For Walter Andrews, one thousand four hundred. . . ."

From there on his rising words were lost in a roar that muffled even the unruly blast of a six-gun someone fired farther down the street. The crowd went wild, shouting madly; hats were thrown in the air, and the hollow explosions of other guns joined the first. The fringes of the crowd melted to the awninged walks as men headed for the town's saloons to celebrate Walt Andrews's victory. Twenty or thirty people mounted the hotel steps below, obviously in search of the new sheriff.

Mace Dow reached over Keyes's shoulder and slammed the window shut and turned and headed for the door to the hall.

"Where to, Mace?" Keyes called out, seeing his lawman's back disappearing into the dimly lit hallway.

"Down to Mike's," was Dow's surly answer. "And if any jasper tries to rub it in on me, Walt Andrews can damn' well make me his first arrest!"

The door slammed with a violence that shook the one faded picture on the room's side wall.

Summers's brows gathered in a studied frown as he gazed at the closed door. "Sometimes I don't understand you, Keyes. Take Dow, for instance. He's. . . ."

"I know. Maybe I'm about through with Mace."

From the narrow alleyway between the two stores across from the hotel, Hugh Conner witnessed the breaking up of the crowd, saw Mace Dow walk spraddle-legged down the steps, and shove his way roughly along the walk to Faro Mike's. Hugh waited two minutes longer, hoping to see Keyes follow Mace.

He smiled and reached down to loosen carefully his guns in their holsters. Then, pulling his Stetson low over his eyes, he went on down the walk in the same direction Mace had taken. He took his time about it, so that it was ten minutes before he crossed the street and shouldered through the batwings of the Palace. Only a dozen men stood at the bar. The tables were nearly deserted, a few percentage girls spotted here and there among the drinkers. The other saloons were getting the play tonight, for Faro Mike had placed his bets on the wrong horse in this race, and this was the pay-off.

Hugh's glances shuttled quickly over the scene before him. Most of these men were Key-Bar riders, and they took their whisky in silence, still awed by the turn of events none of them had expected. The lamps glowed dully from their brackets in the ceiling and the walls, penetrating the thick smoke haze to give the room a blue, foggy look.

Hugh smiled thinly. If it had been arranged especially for his purpose, things couldn't have been nicer. Mace Dow stood bellied to the bar, talking with Faro Mike over the counter. Mike was a slick-haired, chinless little man outfitted in a black coat and tie and a pink shirt that matched his untanned skin. Just now his beady eyes glanced toward the swing doors, and he caught sight of Hugh and spoke quickly to Mace.

The ex-sheriff turned slowly, propped his elbows on the bar, and faced Hugh. His gesture was a signal for silence. Others had seen it, and with one or two exceptions they were Wyatt Keyes's friends and had no love for Hugh.

Across the hush of the room, Mace said: "Look who's here!"

Faro Mike put in his word: "Get out, Conner! Get out before I have you thrown out!" He nodded significantly to three men standing at the end of the bar, men whose breadth of shoulder and thick chests and arms named them for what they were, Mike's bouncers.

"I don't think I will," Hugh replied. "Mike, I'm goin' to take your place apart. Mace, I'm goin' to take you apart."

On the heel of his words he let his right hand flow up smoothly and palm out a heavy Colt. Mace had seen the beginning of that move and sent his two hands stabbing down at his guns, but Hugh's weapon suddenly thundered into the silence, and a chip flew from the molding of Mike's shiny bar less than half an inch from Mace's down-swinging right wrist. He took his hands from his sides as though someone had prodded him in the back with a loaded shotgun.

To one side of Dow, behind him and at the rear wall, Hugh saw a man he recognized as Shorty Crowe of the Key-Bar edge cautiously behind his neighbor. Hugh swung his Colt around and thumbed a shot that slapped into the weathered board alongside Shorty's hat brim. The man in front threw himself flat on his

24

face, exposing Shorty with his hand closed on gun butt. He let go of the handle of his weapon as though it had suddenly become a white-hot iron, calling out stridently: "Lay off, Conner! Swing your cutter away!"

Hugh sauntered across until he stood six feet in front of Mace: "Had enough, lawman?"

Mace glared, but made no answer, speechless in his humiliation. Abruptly Hugh reached out with his left hand and took hold of the sheriff's badge on Mace's shirt pocket and brought his hand down in a sudden motion that ripped the other's shirt wide open: "Your turn's over, Mace. Go back to cow-nursin'!"

At the limits of his vision Hugh saw Faro Mike make a stealthy move with one hand beneath the bar. Tossing the sheriff's badge on the bar top, he reached quickly for a tin tray used by the barkeeps for serving drinks to the tables. He took it by its rim and with a flick of the wrist sailed it into the mirror behind Mike. It whirled true, knocking down a row of bottles and a mound of glasses before it crashed into the mirror.

Mike straightened from his crouch and raised his arms to protect himself from the flying glass, knocking a double-barreled shotgun from its hangers under the bar. Hugh laughed mirthlessly: "Go ahead, Mike, pick it up."

The creak of the swing-door hinges up front cut in on Hugh's words. He jerked his head around in time to see Walt Andrews step through the doors and stop, his brown eyes wide in amazement. Andrews was seeing a crowd of men with upthrust hands standing quietly along the far wall, the bar mirror wrecked, and the place filling with the stench of spilled whisky, Mace Dow with his torn shirt, and Hugh Conner with a Colt held steadily in his hand, leaning carelessly back against the bar as though unmindful of the twenty men facing him.

Bull Forks' new sheriff tried not to smile, yet his inner amusement was betrayed in the warm light that crept into his brown eyes. He said: "Put up your gun and come along with me, Hugh."

In answer he got a brief shake of the head. Hugh moved the snout of his weapon two inches, until it covered the lawman. "Not tonight, Sheriff. Not any other night. I'm leavin' the country." He reached around and picked up the badge he had torn from Mace Dow's shirt and tossed it across so that it lit at Andrew's feet. "Pin it on, Sheriff. I'm wishin' you luck with it."

Walt Andrews looked down at the badge. He didn't pick it up. Instead, he reached into a back pocket of his Levi's, slowly, so that Hugh wouldn't misunderstand the move. He brought his hand out and tossed something back at Hugh—an object that flashed as it reflected the light of the hanging lamps overhead and lit with a ringing sound at Hugh's feet. Hugh looked down, saw a five-pointed star with DEPUTY SHERIFF lettered across its face.

"Pin it on, Hugh. Maybe between us we can make our own brand of luck." Then, without waiting for

Hugh to answer, Andrews's face went serious again, and he looked across at Faro Mike and said: "This place is to be closed at midnight, and every night from now on, Mike. My deputy here will be around to see to it. Hugh, if this place is open at one minute past twelve, wreck it like you wanted. Come over to my office and I'll swear you in."

III

Last night Hugh had listened to Walt Andrews with suspicion. He'd gone out of the Palace with Bull Forks' new sheriff and down to the jail, still thinking that before the night was over he'd go to the deserted lean-to in the alley where his claybank was hidden and climb into the saddle and ride away.

But Andrews was an honest man and showed it. "The girl told me about it, Hugh. George Baird's girl. I reckon I owe the two of you a heap more than I can ever pay back. But I can try, and I'm startin' now. I need a good deputy, and you look like the right man . . . just like Fay Baird said you would. Here, lift your right hand and repeat these words after me. . . ."

This morning, having had a few hours' sleep at the hotel after a night spent mainly in quieting drunks too full of election-day whisky, Hugh Conner was again a little awed at the turn of events. Instead of being on his way to hide from the law, he was wearing a law badge and would someday probably read a Reward dodger with his own name on it. He didn't have to ask himself what had made him take Andrews's offer. It was Fay Baird, the knowledge that she needed him. She had found Walt Andrews a deputy.

Turning in at the jail office walk, Hugh saw a buckboard at the hitch rail in front. The horses were jaw-branded Chain Link. He hesitated about going in, thinking that the girl might be in there with Andrews. Just then the sheriff opened the door and called out: "Hugh you're needed in here!"

George Baird was Andrews's only visitor. He nodded a greeting to Hugh, and the sheriff said: "George has brought me some news, Hugh. You'd better hear it."

"You tell him, Walt," Baird said. The Chain Link owner was a man of Andrews's generation, turning fifty, massive and with a deep, powerful voice and outfitted exactly like the men who worked for him— Levi's, cotton shirt, buffalo coat, worn boots, and a faded gray Stetson. He wore no guns. Hugh knew about that—Baird's hatred of guns—and couldn't understand it. Baird had lived by those guns twenty years ago, when they had helped him carve his small empire out of this wild country. But, like many successful men, George Baird argued against the very things that had brought him his success. He had put his guns away years ago, claiming that a man who couldn't get what he wanted by peaceable means in these quiet days was nothing better than an outlaw. The day for guns was past. Perhaps this philosophy was his reason for backing down to Wyatt Keyes last summer and losing ten sections of his choice range.

Just now Walt Andrews cleared his throat and told Hugh: "We've all been wonderin' what Keyes wanted of that valley up your way, Hugh. The man's got more room than he needs, and it seemed damned unreasonable to drive out a bunch of small ranchers and squatters just to fence in more. This mornin' George heard something that may tell us."

"Now don't get me wrong, Walt," Baird hastened to interrupt. "I don't say it means a thing. I don't want to start any hard feelings with Wyatt Keyes."

Andrews frowned. "If anyone starts anything with Keyes, it'll be me or Hugh. George, damn it, when are you goin' to rare onto your hind legs and stand up for your rights?"

"That has nothing to do with this, Walt. Suppose you tell Conner what you started to."

Andrews checked his rise of temper and turned to Hugh again. "George stayed at the hotel last night. This mornin', comin' down to breakfast, he saw Keyes talkin' with a stranger, a city man. They hadn't heard him come down the stairs, and, as George walked past the desk, he heard this stranger tell Keyes . . . 'Get up there today and find out for sure. And remember, don't send Mace Dow. You're through with him or I'm through.' Now what do you make of that, Hugh?"

"A stranger?" Hugh mused. "Tellin' Keyes he was through with Mace?" He shrugged. "I can't make anything of it."

"I can," the lawman said. "I think this jasper was talkin' about sendin' Mace up to the valley to dicker with those people who won't sell to Keyes. Something's goin' on around here we ought to know about, Hugh. Suppose you loaf around the hotel today and see what you can pick up about the stranger. See where's he's from, what he's doin', who he works for. There won't be much else doin' day after election."

Hugh got up out of his chair and started for the door.

"Another thing, Conner," Baird said. "I saw Keyes later, and he swears he didn't fire your place yesterday."

Hugh grinned broadly. "Ask the sheriff about that." He left the office.

Baird looked at his friend. "Well, Walt?"

Andrews's face had taken on a tide of deeper color. "Hell, George, you might as well know. Hugh fired his own place. Fay saw him do it from where she was watchin' up above his pasture. They cooked up this yarn between 'em, after Keyes and Dow had made a try at kickin' Hugh off his place. It's what put me in office."

"You mean Fay lied to me?"

"She didn't. She told the truth . . . but just enough to suit her."

"But. . . ." Baird was choked with indignation. "Why would she deceive me? Why would she . . . ?"

"Because she knows you, George. Because she knew you'd spoil her play. Because she wants to get you riled up so you'll start packin' your guns again and use 'em on Keyes the next time he tramples on you. Hell, George, there was a time when you'd spit in a range bull's eye if he looked sideways at you. I'd like to see you in this same frame of mind again. Don't think Keyes is through with you. In five more years he aims to take over your place as one of his line camps, the way things are goin'."

Baird stood up, his lips pressed so tightly together that they had turned white. "I never thought I'd hear that sort of talk from you, Walt."

"You'll hear that and plenty more," Andrews stubbornly insisted. "And when you're at home, Fay is goin' to ride you double-rigged. George, Wyatt Keyes has something up his sleeve. When he gets ready to show his hand, I'll need every friend I've got. And when that time comes, I aim to see you swingin' a pair of cutters at your hips. Now if you're sore, go outside and cool off. I've spoken my piece, and I feel a lot better for it."

Baird stomped out of the office, his massive body squarely erect, his chin set stubbornly. Walt Andrews chuckled as the door slammed. Maybe he'd given his friend too big a bite to chew all at once. "But he can handle it," he growled. "George hasn't got store teeth, and, when he swallows that piece, he may find out he's got some guts to digest it."

Gerald P. Summers was a cautious man. Instead of loafing in the lobby throughout the day, he kept to his room, out of sight. He didn't welcome this prolonged stay in Bull Forks, cooped up in a hotel room, but in the past he had put himself to even greater discomfort for less money, and it had taught him patience. Tonight, late probably, Wyatt Keyes would be in with definite word of the progress he had made in the valley during the day. Tomorrow noon Summers would be on his way to Denver with a full report for the directors. Looking forward to that meeting, he permitted himself a satisfied smile at the thought that soon, very soon, he would be one of them; the Sierra Central was progressive enough to reward a man's efforts.

He ate his noon meal in a corner of the nearly deserted dining room, knowing that he could get better food at any one of the three lunchrooms down the street, but not wanting to run the risk of making himself too conspicuous. As he started back to his room, he had a thought that made him turn and go over to the desk. He borrowed a sheet of paper from the clerk and stood there, writing for a full minute. Then he folded the paper, went upstairs, got his hat, and came down and went out the front door.

He walked unhurriedly to the first corner, turned down a side street, and after a hundred yards crossed the railroad tracks and turned in at the station. Inside, he said to the man behind the wicket—"Get this off right away."—and tossed two silver dollars onto the counter. He got his change, and went straight back to his room at the hotel to read a three-day-old Denver paper.

Hugh had followed him. He waited for five minutes before he crossed the rutted street and went into the station. He found the station agent in his cubbyhole office, straightening some papers on the desk beside his telegraph key. The headphone to the instrument hung at his neck; he was getting ready to send a message.

He turned at Hugh's entrance, grinned broadly, and said: "They tell me you're doin' over the Palace, Conner."

Hugh smiled and breathed a little hard, as though he had been running. "It's gettin' so a gent can't have any more fun in this town." Then: "I'm in time, I see. You haven't sent it yet?"

"Sent what?"

"That message my friend just brought in. He wanted to change a word or two. He was busy, so I offered to come down here for him."

As Hugh spoke, a flicker of suspicion edged into the agent's glance. But when the explanation was complete, he reached around and took a sheet of paper from beside his instrument and pushed it through the wicket. "Here it is. I haven't even read it yet. You got a pencil?"

Hugh shook his head, and the agent reached up for the pencil behind his ear and gave it to Hugh.

The message read:

S.M. Hornblow, President, Sierra Central Railroad Offices, Hulbert and Clark Streets, Denver,

Colorado. Business to be concluded tonight. Everything looks favorable for delivery of deeds in three weeks' time. Will give full report at meeting Friday. G. P. Summers.

Hugh scratched out the word "Friday" and wrote "Saturday" above it, handing it back through the wicket again along with the pencil. "Much obliged. Hurry and get it off."

As he turned away, the agent looked down at the message and asked: "Is the road buyin' some property?"

Hugh shrugged. "As near as I can make out, they're runnin' a spur up from Colgate to that coal mine beyond Cow Creek. They're havin' a little trouble gettin' a right-of-way. Don't mention it, though."

"Not me."

Hugh took his time about getting back to the sheriff's office, wanting to digest the facts he had gathered. Summers's wire was easily readable along with the few facts he already knew. It was plain that Summers and Keyes were working together to get control of the valley, probably for a right-of-way. The Sierra Central's main line came through Bull Forks, had been put through four years ago, and had been unprofitable from many standpoints. Traffic to the west was light, and three bad years had seen the ranchers shipping little beef to the East. But over the mountains, to the north, lay a rich, protected valley that ran along the jagged peaks of the Saw Tooth range for nearly a hundred miles. As yet no railroad had

34

touched it, chiefly because the cost of running a line over the mountains had so far been prohibitive. But Hugh knew now that the Sierra Central had found a way—through the pass that lay at the head of the valley where he had lived these past few months. What was Keyes getting out of it? He thought he knew. Summers and Keyes were in together to get the land cheaply, and Keyes was being paid for his work. *Paid lots, or he wouldn't be in it*, Hugh mused. Then he remembered the telegram, its veiling of the truth, and the logical answer came to him, that somehow G.P. Summers—who was registered at the hotel as H. Riley of Carson, Nevada—was also in this for money. *If he can buy it up for a song, he'll have a nice piece of change left over.*

The thing was amazingly simple, so simple that he hesitated in believing that he had discovered the truth. He hurried his steps a little, wanting to tell Andrews what he had learned. Between them they should be able to think this out.

It was the small, six-section outfit at the head of the valley that presented the biggest problem. Keyes had known it from the first—that old Ben White would be a hard nut to crack. Now, as he sat on White's porch and looked across at the aging cattleman sitting in a chair at the other side of the door, he was somehow amused to think that such a small stumbling block threatened the whole scheme he and Summers had so carefully worked out.

"You say you're comfortable here, that you don't need money, that you won't sell. What would you say to a hundred dollars a section for movin' out if I'd give you six sections of my best grass in exchange? The money would be clear profit, and you'd be down out of the winter."

White leaned forward in his chair, took a bit-chewed pipe from his mouth, and spit out across the railing, running the back of his hand beneath his corn-silk mustache as he settled back in his seat again. "Keyes, I've sat up here for ten years watchin' you Bull Forks ranchers fight it out among you. I've saved a little, had a lot of satisfaction out of bein' where I was. I heer tell how Walt Andrews won the election yesterday. That's the way it ought to be. You've been ridin' too wide and too high to suit me. You can't give a good reason for wantin' this place, which looks queer. If you gave me a gold-plated saddle and the finest six sections of your range, I wouldn't stir for a thousand a section. It's a fact, I think you're tryin' to pull a forked deal here. You can get out any time you feel like it."

Without a further word, White got up from his chair and stalked inside his house. He had spoken with an old man's tempered bitterness, in a passionless state-ment-of-fact manner that was eloquently contemp-tuous to Keyes. He left Keyes with a fevered flush suf-fusing the Key-Bar owner's face and neck, and a speechless anger keeping him rooted in his chair. Alone on the porch, in the full view of the three riders who had come up here with him and were waiting at the far limits of the hard-packed yard, Keyes felt like a fool.

He got up finally, sauntered off down the steps, and walked over to his horse, trying to hide the rage that had taken hold of him. "We'll ride," he said curtly, and went up into the saddle. He led his men two miles down the valley, then, without any announcement of his intention, he cut off across a park-like meadow and took to a little used trail that wound up and over a hummock through the cedars. On the far side, he drew rein beside the pool of a clear-watered spring and climbed down out of the saddle and announced briefly: "We stay here till after dark."

Dusk came in less than an hour. He silently watched his men build a fire and cook a meal, running over in his mind the things he had done so far to help Summers. Today he had jolted Mace by telling him he was no longer needed on this business, but could have his old job of foreman back again. Mace had been a fool, and he was glad to be rid of him. The thing was too big to let a man like White stand in his way. Thirty thousand dollars was involved here, and the job was three-quarters finished. Hugh Conner was another stumbling block, but Keyes already knew how to take care of him. With old man White and Hugh Conner out of the way, he could end this in a hurry. The main thing was the need of ending the deal at once, before too many people became suspicious. There was the burning of Conner's lay-out as clear proof that someone already suspected what was going on. Had Conner touched off that blaze himself?

No, the man was too stubborn to burn the roof over his head when he could stay and fight.

After he had eaten, Keyes spoke to his men: "You three were hired at a hundred a month, and I told you it was fightin' wages. Tonight I'll prove that. We're ridin' back to White's place."

He eyed them individually, Slim with his unreadable thin face and cold, caramel-colored eyes; Tony, whose long nose and full lips gave a hint of his Indian ancestry; and Blazer, whose huge body dwarfed the other two and whose ugly, pockmarked face and ham-like fists and brawny strength had made him a killer before turning fifteen. Keyes knew his men and now told them: "Whatever happens tonight puts us all in the same buggy. I don't think I'll have to worry about any of you talkin'."

"Let's get on with it," Blazer growled, voicing the opinion of the others.

An hour later Keyes looked down on Ben White's place, shadowy in the star-lit darkness. He waited impatiently, watching the cabin's single lighted window, wondering how long it would take Blazer to make the first move.

It came sooner than he expected, a hoarse, piercing cry from out of the trees in front of the cabin. Keyes transferred his glance to the cobalt-shadowed porch, waiting for the one happening that was beyond his control. When the door opened to throw a shaft of orange light out over the porch and the yard, he breathed a sigh of relief.

It was better than he had hoped for. Ben White came out of his door, holding a lighted lantern high over his head, peering out into the light.

"Who's there?" White called out, and the words were hardly out of his mouth before Tony's shape darted into the circle of light behind him. White's choked, startled cry drifted out across the night and his knees suddenly buckled and he dropped the lantern, snuffing out its light so that only the duller glow of lamplight from inside brought out the details. Tony caught the rancher as he fell, and lifted and dragged him in through the door, out of sight.

Slim appeared out of the darkness and walked across the porch and into the cabin, shutting the door behind him. Inside, he helped Tony lift White, whose eyes were already glazing, to his bunk. They took off his boots and threw his blankets over him, and Slim even thought to take the rancher's pipe out of his pocket and put it on the chair alongside the bunk.

Tony brought the lamp over and set it on the chair. Then, giving it a gentle shove, he watched it topple to the floor with a crash as both base and chimney shattered. The wick guttered out, so Slim wiped a match alight on the seat of his trousers and flicked it into the spreading pool of coal oil. The flame caught in a pungent, black cloud of smoke, then spread and licked up along the blankets until they suddenly burst into flame.

"That'll do," Slim said, watching Tony wipe the blood off his knife on a corner of the blankets. "Walk on your toes on the way out and stick to the path. The boss said we weren't to leave tracks."

"Not my tracks!" Tony breathed, and made his way across the wavily lighted room to the door.

They met the others on the trail below.

"Everything all right?" Keyes queried, as they swung in alongside his pony.

Slim grinned. "Slick as a whistle, boss."

IV

At twenty minutes past nine that same night Walt Andrews took out his watch and looked at it, and then across his office at his deputy. "It's time," he said. "You've got the horses saddled? You're sure he doesn't know you?"

Hugh nodded, and got up out of his chair. "He doesn't. On the way back I thought I'd like to swing up into the valley to my place. I forgot and left the corral shut. Those bronc's ought to be on the loose until I get back up there for good."

"Go ahead. There won't be anything doin' around here in the mornin'."

Hugh left the office, and for two full minutes Walt Andrews sat staring at the door, elbows on the arms of his chair, one hand slowly fingering his grizzled mustache. At length he reached down and opened a drawer beside him and took out a sheaf of Reward posters and fingered through them until he found the one he wanted. He put it on the desk before him and returned the others to the drawer. For the tenth time that day he read that poster.

He gave a long, subdued sigh and abruptly rose and crumpled the dodger and took it over to the stove, raising the lid and dropping it onto the hot coals inside. Then he came back to the desk and sat down and laboriously penciled a note that was addressed to a Montana sheriff and read: *Have you further information to add to Reward notice dated March of this year regarding killer of Wade Henderson?* Finished, he reached to the peg on the wall behind his desk and took down his Stetson and put it on. He banked the fire in the stove, opened the check draft, blew out the lamp and went outside. On his way to the station to send his telegram, he looked in through the hotel doors. Hugh Conner was talking to the oldster behind the desk.

Hugh was saying: "Is Riley in?"

The clerk nodded. "Room Twenty."

Hugh went on up the steps. He knocked at the door of Room 20 and heard a chair scrape inside. Then Summers's voice queried: "Who is it?"

"Keyes sent me."

The door opened, and Summers stood there with a gun in his hand, but hanging at his side. He jerked his head, and Hugh stepped in, closing the door behind him.

"Were you expectin' Mace Dow?" Hugh asked, grinning as he observed the wicked-looking, short-barreled gun Summers carried.

Summers nodded: "How did you know?"

Instead of answering the question, Hugh voiced another guess: "That's why I came. About Mace, I mean. He's been proddy all day because he didn't get taken along. Keyes thought you ought to be movin' out of here to a safer place."

"You mean that Mace . . . ?"

"I mean that it would be easy for Mace to crawl onto that roof outside and blow a hole through you if he wanted. He's ornery."

Summers's eyes became narrow-lidded, flared with suspicion. "Who are you? What do you know?"

"All there is to know. You're Summers of the Sierra Central, and the boss is helpin' you swing a deal for buyin' up the valley that leads to that low pass up by Wind River. Isn't that enough?"

Summers laughed, not heartily, for he had been put under a terrific strain in the last minute. "What does Keyes want me to do?"

"Get your stuff packed, leave money on the table for your room, and come along with me. We'll go down the back way. I've got two ponies waitin' out in the alley. We'll get out of town without anyone seein' you and let Mace do what he likes about it."

Summers worked quickly, packing his belongings in his one bag. He left a five-dollar gold piece on the bureau, blew out the lamp, and they went down the back stairs. When they had ridden down the alley to its end and were suddenly in open country, the town behind, Summers queried: "Where are you taking me?"

"It's a long ride. You'll see."

After two hours of steady going along the trail that angled south and east from Bull Forks, Summers shifted uncomfortably in his saddle and asked impatiently: "How much farther?"

"Another hour."

They rode on in silence for a while, until Hugh said abruptly: "There's some of us who don't think we're getting enough out of this deal. Take Mace, for instance. Keyes has used him for fifteen years, and now he throws him down like a worn-out pair of boots."

The one thing Hugh had to go on was what George Baird had overheard Summers say that morning and the belief that Wyatt Keyes had gone a little too far in using Mace, and that doubtless he regretted it now. A man like Keyes wouldn't waste time trying to swing an understrapper into line, for it was a simple matter to find a man to rod an outfit like the Key-Bar efficiently.

"Keyes never should have trusted Mace," Summers said. Then, silent a moment, he queried: "Did Keyes give you any word to bring to me?"

"Only to get back to Denver as quick as you can and to wait to hear from him."

"Back to Denver?"

Hugh nodded, pointed ahead to where a half-dozen pinpoints of light winked out in the distance. "That's Colgate. I'm to see that you leave on the midnight train."

"But this. . . ." Summers stubbornly clamped his jaw shut after those two words. It was a full five minutes later that he said: "Keyes wouldn't be fool enough to try to reach me by wire. I've warned him about that. He'd lay the whole thing wide open if he did. All wires come direct to the office, and a copy is put on open file. I'd be cashiered the minute it was delivered. I'm supposed to be down here doing this on my own."

Hugh looked across at the man, saw the beads of perspiration standing out on his forehead. He chuckled softly and said: "I wouldn't worry."

But Summers did worry. While they waited in the gloomy shed that served as the Colgate way station, he penciled a note that he gave Hugh to deliver to Keyes.

Forty minutes later they flagged the train, using the red lantern that hung inside the shed for that purpose. Summers climbed onto the last coach, pausing on the step long enough to tell Hugh: "There's something I forgot to mention. If that man White wouldn't sell today, tell Keyes to double the two-hundred-dollar limit. We'll split the loss between us."

The locomotive cut loose with two sharp blasts of its whistle, and the coaches started moving. Hugh's last look at the man showed him a face robbed of its color wearing a pallid, worried tenseness.

When the lantern swinging from the end of the last coach had faded into the darkness, Hugh opened the note Summers had given him. He flicked alight a match and held it over the scrap of paper, reading:

In case you want to reach me, wire my sister, Miss Anne Summers, 27 County Hotel, Denver. This business must be finished by the end of next week, otherwise I advise Sierra Central to use their option on the lower pass before it expires.

G. Summers

With that last bit of information Hugh pieced together the final links of this chain of circumstances damning Wyatt Keyes.

One remark of Summers's stayed in his mind. *"If that man White wouldn't sell today tell Keyes to double the two-hundred-dollar limit."* That would be Ben White, up at the head of the valley. So Ben had been stubborn?

Knowing Keyes and his ways, Hugh felt a vague alarm over this news. If Ben White wouldn't sell, then Keyes would use other means. Why not ride up and have a talk with Ben and warn him? So thinking, Hugh tied the reins of Summer's horse to the saddle horn and led the animal a half mile down the Bull Forks road before he turned him loose. Then he cut north from the trail with an all-night ride ahead of him.

If Hugh thought he and Summers had left the hotel unseen, he was mistaken. Mace, who had been drinking all day at Faro Mike's after Keyes's curt order to report at the Key-Bar the following day, had been on his way across the street to the lunchroom for a late supper when he saw Hugh, entering the hotel. Sight of the man who was chiefly responsible for his falling from Keyes's good graces brought up a killing lust within Mace. He followed Hugh into the hotel and asked the clerk where he had gone.

When the oldster had answered—"He's up in Room Twenty with Riley."—Mace had given way to his disbelief for one instant, and then realized fully what this meant. Here was a way to buy back into Keyes's favor once more!

He went into the upper hallway and hid in the shadow of the stairwell until Hugh and Summers left the room. He followed them down into the alley and out of town. He went back for his horse and made a wide circle to the Colgate trail and saw them ride past an hour later. Two hours after that, he hunkered down in a mesquite thicket less than twenty yards from the station and saw Hugh flag the midnight train. After the train pulled out, he watched while Hugh read the note by the light of the match. Twenty minutes after Hugh turned Summers's horse loose on the Bull Forks trail, Mace overtook the animal.

For a long ten seconds a cold fear took hold of him at the thought that Hugh might have seen him and be waiting along the trail ahead. But then he reasoned that, if Hugh had discovered his presence and was waiting, he wouldn't have left this pony in the trail as a warning.

He rode past the riderless broncho, putting his own animal into a swinging run, muttering: "Goddlemighty, will Wyatt be glad to see me this time!"

46

V

It was an hour after sunup when Hugh rounded the head of the trail to look on Ben White's place. A neat two-room cabin had stood proudly in the niche the thick cedars made against the abrupt slope of the hills up ahead. But now that cabin was gone, and in its place was a pile of charred, smoking timbers that was mute evidence of what had happened.

Hugh felt something within him harden and turn cold. It was a full half minute before he put down the nausea that gripped him and spurred up the trail, to where a man stood looking down at him from alongside the cabin's ruins.

He knew what he would find even before he asked the man, Jeff Wilke, White's nearest neighbor: "What happened, Jeff?"

Wilke was a bear-like man, thick-framed, short, and with a bushy black beard that gave him a pugnacious look even though he was mild-mannered and soft-spoken. He lifted his sloping shoulders in a shrug. "I wouldn't know, Hugh. I spotted this blaze at eight or thereabouts last night. Me and the missus hitched up the team and drove here as fast as we could. It was blazin' like a stack o' dry hay. Hell, we couldn't've got in to him if we had known!"

"He was in there?"

Wilke nodded, and turned to let his glance run over the burned, upended line of timber lengths that marked the remains of the partition dividing the cabin into its two rooms. "We've had a look, Hugh. It wasn't nice. As near as we could make out, old Ben went to sleep with the lamp burnin'. It tipped off his chair. He's in what's left of his bunk. There's a couple of legs left of the chair, near the bunk. His blanket was over him because he was layin' on part of 'em . . . the part that didn't burn. His pipe was there alongside the chair . . . the only damned thing that's supposed to burn and didn't. You can take a look, if you want, but you won't eat for a week if you do."

Hugh swung down out of the saddle and had a look around the yard. "Anyone come up here yesterday or last night?"

"Keyes and three of his hardcases was up here to have a talk with Ben. I know, because they stopped at my place, and Keyes paid me my money and told me he aimed to call on Ben."

"Then you sold out?"

"What the hell else could a man do? Keyes has ways of makin' us sell. I'm a family man, Hugh, and I don't aim to mix in with what I can see comin' for those who don't jump at the crack of his whip."

"Was Ben going to sell?"

"He wasn't. He told me so two, three days ago." Wilke frowned, as the gradual dawning of an idea took root in his mind. "Say! Do you figure Keyes came back and . . . ?"

"I don't figure a thing."

Wilke's look turned from worried perplexity to a

grim soberness. "I sent Johnny Davis in after the sheriff. Maybe we ought to get a bunch together and ride over to the Key-Bar."

Hugh shook his head. "And what good would that do us without proof? No, what I want you to do is to keep everyone away from the place until Walt Andrews gets here. I'm ridin' down to my corral to turn some stock loose. I'll be back. You're in charge here while I'm gone. Have you got a gun?"

Wilke swept his sheepskin aside, exposing the cedar-handled butt of a six-gun he had thrust in the waistband of his trousers. "I've been carryin' this for a week now."

"There'll be others comin' along to see what happened as soon as the news gits around. Keep 'em away until Andrews has a chance to look over the cabin and the yard. And you might be careful about spreadin' your tracks around, Jeff. I don't think we'll get much from sign, but there's always a chance."

Hugh mounted and rode on down the trail. He began to feel a slow weariness settling through him and abruptly realized how little rest he had had in the past three days. Excitement had supplied him with the energy for last night's ride, but now he was dog-tired.

"Keyes did it," he muttered, half aloud. Yet as firmly as the conviction took hold of him, just as firmly did he know that there would be no evidence, no proof the law could get to warrant an arrest. The word of the Key-Bar riders would carry as much weight before law, probably more, than any amount of weak evidence the sheriff could supply. Keyes had covered his tracks well.

A half hour later he approached the spot where he had met Fay Baird two days ago, the margin of trees that circled the upper end of his pasture. Remembrance of her was somehow refreshing. After all, his being in on this was a thing of her doing. The girl had fire, probably a measure of those same qualities of her father's that had gone to seed during the past few years. Just now he felt a grim hopelessness at realizing that someday soon he might have to be leaving this country—outriding the law as he had done once before. His luck couldn't hold.

He was leaving the trees and heading down into his pasture when a voice suddenly rang out close at hand: "Conner!"

He stiffened in his saddle and dropped his right hand to his side as he turned to search out that voice. Wyatt Keyes stood thirty feet away, his back to the trunk of a tall cedar, a rifle half raised to his shoulder.

"Look behind you before you make a try for it," Keyes warned tonelessly.

A strange and pervading sense of defeat had already gripped Hugh as he turned and looked to his other side. Mace Dow and the stolid, burly Blazer had ridden out of the trees, each holding a six-gun that was lined at him.

"Shuck out your irons, Conner! One at a time!"

Hugh was careful to time his motions to an agonizing slowness, knowing the men who faced him.

When his guns were on the ground, Keyes said: "Slim, come on out and tie him on."

A fourth man appeared, a stranger to Hugh. The grin on his thin face was belied by the brittle quality in his peculiar, light-colored eyes. He stepped out with a rope in his hands, and stooped over and flicked the noosed end of it onto Hugh's right boot. Then Hugh rolled out of the saddle.

A gun crashed out behind him, searing a burn along his left shoulder. He reached down and his two hands closed on Slim's neck as his weight crashed down on the man. He chopped in a hard blow that caught Slim behind the ear, then groped down wildly to reach the man's holstered six-gun.

His fingers closed on the handle, and he swung the gun clear and thumbed back the hammer and met Blazer's rush with a blasting shot that stopped the man and sent him sinking in a loose sprawl to the ground. Hugh looked around, saw Keyes, and was swinging the weapon into line when Mace Dow's chopping down-stroke from behind wiped the barrel of a six-gun across his temples in a bone-crushing blow that sent him into unconsciousness.

Fay Baird and her father were in Walt Andrews's office that morning when Johnny Davis rode in with the news of Ben White's death.

Andrews took it stoically, frowning as Johnny finished. "Any idea how it started, Johnny?"

"Only that busted lamp alongside his bunk."

"Anyone up there last night?"

"Only Jeff Wilke. He was too late."

"I mean was there anyone up there to see Ben before it happened?"

"Keyes and two or three of his men rode past my place early in the afternoon."

Andrews's eyes took on a granite-like quality. He got up out of his chair and reached for his hat and looked at George Baird and said: "You comin'?"

"Of course, he is," Fay Baird answered, rising to follow the sheriff.

"Wait a minute, Walt," Baird called out. "Why should we go up there with you?"

Andrews's look was one of disgust. "You mean you can't guess the answer?"

With a flush of color rising in under his tan, George Baird said quietly: "You'll have to prove it to me, Walt."

Out on the walk, as they were climbing into their saddles, a man called out from down the street: "Walt, here's a wire for you." It was the station agent. He came up and handed a telegram to Walt Andrews, asking: "Any answer?"

The lawman tore open the message, let the hint of a satisfied smile break in on his sober expression as he read the message, then tucked it into his pocket and said: "No answer, Wade."

They left town at a fast trot and rode that way for nearly two hours, until, at noon, they swung into sight of Hugh's place in the valley. When Andrews saw the three ponies in the corral, he frowned and told Fay, who was riding beside him: "That's funny. He said he'd be up here this mornin'."

He got down out of the saddle and swung open the corral gate and let the horses out to water. Looking up at the ruins of the cabin and wagon shed, he smiled thinly and remarked: "Hugh did a good job of it." Then he turned to Davis. "Johnny, if you can spare the time, I'd like you to wait here for Hugh. Bring him on up to White's if he gets here in the next hour or two."

Davis nodded: "I ain't got a thing to do, Walt. Go ahead."

At White's they met Jeff Wilke. He gave them the story he had given Hugh earlier that morning, and ended by saying: "Hugh ought to be back any minute. He rode on down to his place to turn his stock out to water."

Walt Andrews, who had been gazing soberly at the ruins of the cabin, whirled to face him. "Hugh's been here this mornin'?"

Wilke nodded, his glance puzzled.

"But we came that way looking for him," Fay Baird protested. She had lost a little color during the last few minutes as she listened to Wilke's story and looked out upon the burned cabin. But now his words brought a flush coursing up over her regular features: "That means, Dad . . . it means something's happened to him! Don't you see, if he started down there . . . ?"

"Wilke, go back to your place and saddle a horse and ride down the valley and get every man you can,"

Walt Andrews said in sudden decision. "Get Johnny Davis. We left him at Hugh's place. We're ridin' for the Key-Bar. You'll meet us there in two hours, if you have to kill your jugheads doin' it." He turned to George Baird. "I'm not askin' you two to ride there with me. There may be trouble, then again I may be makin' a wrong guess. But if anything's happened to Hugh, it's an even bet Keyes is mixed up in it."

It wasn't Baird who answered, but his daughter. "I'm coming, Walt. And I think Dad will, too." She cast a sidelong glance at her father, wondering what his answer would be.

George Baird's leathery countenance had undergone a change during the past few months. There was a hard light in his eyes that his daughter had never before seen, but that Walt Andrews remembered from years ago. The lawman smiled grimly, said: "I'd have walked up here on my hands to see you come around, George."

Baird reached around and undid the flap of his saddlebag and took out a long-barreled Colt .38 and rammed it into his belt. When they rode back down the trail, he was leading the way at a stiff run.

The Key-Bar bunkhouse was long and low, a native adobe house converted to Keyes's use. A crude pine table and four benches took up the room's center, while a double tier of bunks, sixteen in all, filled the entire length of the back wall. They threw Hugh Conner into one of these, his hands and feet laced together. Mace and Keyes and Slim had brought him in.

Outside, a man's steps sounded running across the yard. A moment later he appeared in the bunkhouse door. "Someone comin' in along the trail, boss."

Keyes said: "You guard the door, Slim. Don't let anyone in. Mace, better come with me."

Keyes rounded the corner of his big stone house and stopped, scanning the faint ribbon of the Bull Forks trail. A half mile away were three riders. "Looks like Andrews and Baird and his girl. Mace, they may know more than we think. You round up the crew and tell 'em to spread through the house and around the bunkhouse. If Andrews tries to make a play, they're to stop him."

Ten minutes later Keyes was standing on the steps of the porch, his smile affable. He looked out at his three visitors. "Get down and come in," he invited.

Baird's look was fixed severely on Keyes, and Andrews was lacking his usual smile. Even the girl's glance was vaguely accusing, so Keyes queried: "Anything wrong?"

"Keyes, I want to take a look through your house," Andrews said. "Hugh Conner disappeared this mornin' on the way between Ben White's place and his own. You reckon you could explain that?"

"You mean do I know where he went, Walt? No."

"I'll have a look, anyway." Andrews swung down out of his saddle. "Come on, George."

"Just a minute!" Keyes said. "You can't go in there, Walt. Not without a search warrant. If you'd come here as friends and wanted a look through the lay-out, you'd be welcome. But when you hang a thing like this on me without reason, when you decide to blame me for every forked play that's made in this country, you aren't welcome. First, you blamed this fire of Conners's onto me. I didn't do it. Now, it's this other. You ride back to town and get yourself a search warrant and I'll listen."

"You wouldn't know about Ben White's bein' killed and his place burned last night, would you, Keyes?"

There wasn't a trace of emotion to betray Keyes. "White's place fired?" He even managed a scornful laugh. "Next you'll be sayin' I did that."

"Keyes, I'm goin' to look this place over whether you like it or not. Come on, George." The sheriff walked toward the porch. George Baird followed, and Keyes stepped aside to let them pass, a smug smile heightening his arrogance.

Andrews turned the knob on the door and threw it open, then stopped. Four feet inside the house's big living room stood a Key-Bar rider with a double-barreled shotgun slung from the crook of his arm. Andrews took one step inside, and the rider silently raised the muzzle of his weapon. Andrews stopped once more and turned to face Keyes. "So that's the way it is?"

Keyes shrugged. "I said you weren't welcome, Walt. Ride back for a search warrant."

56

Baird, more impulsive than his friend, pushed past Walt and into the room. The man with the gun put one hand around the stock, the other on the barrel grip of the shotgun and lined it at Baird and breathed: "Don't make me let this thing off, friend."

"Hold on, George," Andrews growled, as he saw Baird's hand start edging toward his six-gun. "There's plenty of time for this. We can always come back."

He took Baird by the arm and led him back to their ground-haltered ponies, and both men went into the saddle. Andrews led the way out of the yard, ignoring Keyes as best he could.

When they were through the pasture gate, Keyes went inside his office. Mace was waiting there. "Let 'em get out of sight over the hill, Mace. Then you take a *pasear* back along the trail and make sure they didn't leave anyone to watch the lay-out. As soon as you're back, you're headed for the north line shack. You'll take Conner up there, and I can let Andrews have his look at this place this afternoon when he gets back from town."

Ten minutes later Mace rode out of the yard. Keyes watched him make a mile-wide circle, inwardly satisfied at the way his ramrod was going about his job. It looked like Mace was coming around. The ex-sheriff had done a nice piece of work last night in following Hugh and Summers to Colgate, and Keyes was thinking that Summers had been wrong, that he wasn't through with Mace, after all. It wasn't every day a man could find an understrapper like Mace—one who would shut his eyes to the right thing and wasn't squeamish about doing a few dirty jobs.

But half an hour later, still standing there on the porch, it took two seconds for Keyes to change his mind about Mace. He saw his ramrod top the far rise along the trail and ride in toward the house, leading another horse. That horse was Fay Baird's chestnut, and even at this distance Keyes could see the girl lying across the withers of Mace's horse, ahead of his saddle. By the time Mace swung into the yard, Keyes was nursing a temper that had taken the color from his face and was making his black eyes narrow-lidded and beady.

Mace smiled crookedly and called out: "Look what I found hunkered down behind a tree up the trail, boss! She wouldn't come along peaceable, so I tied her up." He swung down, and lifted the girl to the ground, steadying her with one hand to keep her from falling. Fay Baird's hands and feet were tied, her hair was mussed, and her clothes were smeared with dust. "She put up a good scrap," Mace said, laughing softly.

Then he saw the look on Keyes's face, and sobered instantly. Keyes came down off the porch and stood in front of his ramrod. "How much have you told her?"

"All there is to know," Fay Baird said, her chin tilted defiantly. "I know you have Hugh Conner here and that you fired Ben White's place. You'll all hang, Wyatt Keyes!"

Keyes's hand flashed out in an open-handed blow that caught Mace full in the mouth. "So you told her," he purred. His right hand closed on the butt of his gun. "I ought to fill your gutless belly with slugs, you sidewinder!"

Mace swallowed hard, fear riding into his glance. "Hold on, boss! I swear I didn't tell her a thing. I just found her up there, watchin' the lay-out, and brought her back like you said. She made all this up."

"But if you had half a brain. . . ." Keyes broke off abruptly, his rage boiling him speechless. At length, he cooled down enough to say: "This is the worst play you could have made. Now they'll know for sure."

He stood a moment, trying to think above the rising urge that made him want to kill Mace Dow. He would take care of Mace later, he reasoned, for with Fay Baird on his hands, not daring to let her go because of what she knew, he might have need of every gun he could get before long. Or maybe he could make a deal with Walt Andrews—a deal that would be an exchange of his life for the girl's. But he'd have to leave the country unless he played his cards right.

A shout from out by the bunkhouse cut in on his thoughts. He looked over there to see a man pointing up the trail. Keyes's glance whipped around to see, far out, a knot of horsemen swinging toward the lay-out in a boil of dust.

"Get her into the bunkhouse along with Conner!" Keyes rasped. "You have one more chance, Mace. Step out o' line and I'll know what to do! Tell Slim and the others to meet me in the office. You stay at the bunkhouse."

Mace picked the girl up and ran awkwardly toward the bunkhouse, while Keyes went into his office.

Two minutes later, looking through a pair of binoculars, he had identified Jeff Wilkes and Johnny Davis in the group of eight riders. Shortly they stopped well out of range, and Wilkes called across. "We saw the girl, Keyes! Turn her loose, or we'll surround the place and smoke you out!"

Keyes didn't bother to shout back an answer. Reason told him that Wilkes and his men would be careful, knowing that something might happen to the girl if they carried out their threat. But the chance was gone now of leaving for the line camp. They were cornered.

But there's the girl and there's the deputy, he mused, walking back into his office. *And Walt Andrews never broke his word to a man. This isn't over yet!*

Hugh had been lying here for ten minutes now, his head aching until the pain of it drove him half mad. He had heard voices outside a few minutes ago—Walt Andrews's and Wyatt Keyes's voices—and he had questioned Slim, who stood guard at the door. Slim would talk, and did, seeming to take a grim satisfaction in turning Hugh's hopelessness to a bottomless despair. So when Mace brought Fay to the bunkhouse and threw her roughly onto the bunk alongside, Hugh knew more than a little of what had gone on.

Mace told Slim: "The boss wants you up at the office. I'll watch these two."

After Slim had left, Hugh heard the girl say: "This about finishes you with Wyatt Keyes, Dow."

Mace whirled to face her, his pent-up anger giving way before a string of oaths. "That'll be enough out of you, sister!"

A moment later Hugh said: "Mace, the two of us could swing this together."

"Swing what?" Mace stopped his restless pacing in front of the door, and the worry that showed on his gaunt face gave Hugh his cue.

"Keyes is through with you, like she says. Why don't you make your own play and leave the country before you get a bullet in the back?"

"Who said Keyes was through with me?"

Fay Baird laughed mockingly—a laugh that brought Mace whirling around in a hot fury to face the sound of her voice.

Hugh spoke before Mace could give vent to the violence that was building up inside him. "I had it straight from Summers that he and Keyes were ready to get rid of you. Is that proof enough?"

"That was yesterday. Today Keyes thinks different."

"Not after you brought me in," Fay said. Somehow, she had caught the drift of Hugh's remarks.

"Mace, I tallied you as bein' wise. A wise man wearin' your boots would clear out. But when you do clear out, I say you and I ought to cash in on this thing."

"You and me? How?"

"What would George Baird pay to get his girl back?"

61

"Hugh!" Fay was incredulous.

"Don't listen to her," Hugh told Mace. "Get what I have to say. Keyes will hold the girl until Walt Andrews and George Baird come to his terms. Keyes may even collect a little money on her . . . to make up for what he's goin' to have to lose now that he can't buy up the valley for the railroad. He'll leave the country. But it's a three to one bet that he won't take care of you, Mace. He may even turn you over to the law."

"You're loco," Mace scoffed. "I know too much about Keyes. I'll talk."

"Then he'll measure you for a pine nightshirt and not take any chances. You're through, Mace." Hugh paused a second, letting his words sink in. "What we ought to do is to get out of here tonight . . . with your help it'll be easy . . . and take the girl and strike north into the hills and make our own deal with Baird and Andrews. With twenty thousand to split between us, we could leave the country and still be ahead of the game."

A shrewd look had crept into Mace's glance. "Supposin'," he said, "just supposin' I'd sell out on Keyes. What makes you think I'd swing you in on it, friend?"

"You'd have to. Neither Baird nor Andrews would deal with you. They don't trust you, Mace. By the time you convinced them you had the girl, Keyes's crew would have hunted you down. But with me in on it, we can finish the whole thing in a day or so . . . while Keyes is still cooped up here. Both the tin star and old man Baird trust me. They'll do what I say. It's worth twenty thousand, Mace. Think it over."

"You go to hell," was Mace's cautious answer, his words belied by the greedy light that came to his eyes. "I always did wonder about you, Conner. You're plenty shifty."

"When I have to be."

They heard steps approaching across the yard, and a moment later Slim appeared in the doorway. "The boss says for me to stay with these two, Mace." Slim's tone was no longer respectful. Keyes had told him a few things.

Mace left without a word, and Hugh lay there for minutes wondering if he had carried his point. Once he rolled onto his side, so that he could look across at Fay. She managed a smile and whispered: "You didn't really mean it, did you, Hugh?"

He laughed softly. "Part of it."

"Which part?"

"Wait and see."

VI

Walt Andrews and George Baird came back from town shortly before dusk. Slim, standing in the doorway, told Hugh and Fay how the sheriff stopped on the crest of the rise up the trail to talk to Jeff Wilke and his men. Later, Andrews came halfway to the house and called to Keyes, and the Key-Bar owner, surrounded by four of his men, walked out and had a long talk with the lawman. Andrews and Baird didn't come back to the house with him.

After supper, when Slim came back on duty, he gave Hugh the news. "Andrews didn't like the boss' proposition. So he's out there, with his posse coverin' the lay-out, tryin' to think of a way to get you two loose." Slim chuckled. "Maybe he'll feel different in the mornin'."

The night wore on slowly for Hugh, for each moment he expected to be hearing from Mace. This was their only chance, and, unless Mace did his part, they might never get out of here alive. Slim, good-natured and obliging, several times rolled cigarettes for Hugh. He wasn't worrying, and Hugh knew that the man reflected Keyes's confidence.

Shortly after ten it happened. Mace came to the door and told Slim: "Time for coffee. The boss says for me to stick around while you're up at the cook shanty. Be back in ten minutes."

Slim hesitated, suspicion flaring in his glance. But finally his eyes lost their hardness, and he gave a thin smile and leaned his rifle against the door frame and sauntered out into the darkness. They listened to the sound of his steps receding across the yard. Then Mace said quickly: "Keyes has got his guards all around this lay-out. Barn, sheds, corral." He stepped over to Hugh and bent down quickly and slashed at his ropes with a knife. Then he crossed over to Fay and had her on her feet in a quarter of a minute. He took out one of his guns, and handed it to Hugh. "We'll cut

64

out back for the wagon shed. There's no time for saddle ponies, so we'll head across that field out back and make for the trees on that far hill."

He turned down the lamp, went to the door and looked out, and then signaled them to follow and disappeared into the darkness outside. Hugh was stiff and sore from lying in one position for so long, and it was several seconds before he could reach out to steady Fay and walk awkwardly to the door with his hand holding her arm. As he went out with her, he reached down and got Slim's rifle. Outside, they walked quickly now, coming closer to the Key-Bar ramrod. Ahead, the bulk of the wagon shed loomed blackly in the shadows.

They heard someone softly call—"Mace?"—and recognized Slim's voice. Mace stiffened and whirled, and the next instant a welling blossom of orange powder flame licked out thirty feet away, punctuating a hollow gun blast that ripped across the yard at Mace. His gun answered the next instant, and they heard a low, throttled groan as his bullet hit Slim. Then Hugh picked up the girl and ran past Mace's weaving figure for the door of the wagon shed.

He set Fay down and jerked open the door and pushed her inside as someone at the far corner of the building called out a strident challenge. Hugh made out the guard's figure and lifted the Colt Mace had given him and thumbed one shot that blasted across the silence. The man's shadowy outline sank to the ground, and Hugh lunged through the door into the building just as other shots crashed out from up by the house. He took one last glimpse out across the yard and saw Mace's lean frame sprawled loosely on the ground twenty feet away. Mace wasn't moving out of that ungainly sprawl. He was dead.

Shouts shuttled out across the still air, and from down by the barn someone with a rifle set up a careful, even firing that whipped lead through the wagon shed's door. As that first bullet splintered the wood sheathing, Hugh flicked alight a match and looked quickly around.

Fay stood ten feet ahead of him, in the center of the shed's open dirt floor. There was a litter of gear strewed along the right-hand side, broken bridles, harness, and a buggy's gaunt chassis backed into a far corner. Along the left-hand wall was stacked a waist-high pile of twelve-inch planks. Hugh's match flickered out, and he lit another and told Fay: "Get down behind that lumber."

He held that light long enough for her to make a place for herself between the lumber and the side wall, then, with one quick look around, he threw the match to the floor as other bullets found the mark of that door.

In his hasty glimpse toward the front he had seen a loose board near the base of the weathered frame wall, far to one side. He felt his way toward it now, once feeling the air whip of a bullet as it tore through the siding and rushed past his face. Finally he found the board and tore it loose and bellied down behind the small opening to look outside.

What he saw made him reach frantically for the rifle at his side. He had barely time to thrust its muzzle through the opening, to take aim, and to fire at the figure darting in out of the darkness at the wagon shed door. The running man outside broke his long stride, and he fell forward, with a momentum that rolled him over twice before he lay still. Hugh had aimed at his chest.

Guns from up by the house set up an inferno of thunder, the low-pitched crashes of six-guns blending discordantly with the sharper explosions of the rifles. They hadn't spotted the opening at the base of the wall yet, but were covering the door with their shots.

Then, from farther away, he heard other guns. He listened for a full half minute, trying to identify those far sounds. Suddenly, from the darkness beyond the house's long, low shadow, he saw a distant wink of flame, then another beside it, and he turned and called back to Fay: "Andrews and your father are in it now!"

"Hugh, you must be careful." It was as though he hadn't mentioned the others.

Her tone, the low, intimate throb of her voice, set up in him a feeling that he had never before experienced. In that moment he knew that Fay Baird meant something more than a friend. Her words, her thoughts, had been for him alone. In those few seconds, he knew that he had found the one thing in life that mattered to him. He had found it and would lose it, for if he came through this night alive, he would have to face the same thing he had been facing for days now, for

67

months—the knowledge that the dark trails held his future, that he could never again live his life the way he would have chosen.

Abruptly the shots from the house died out. In a few moments the rifles of the posse that had been throwing a steady fire at the house stopped firing, lacking the target of the gunfire flashes.

Through the existing silence, Keyes's voice sounded from the near side of the house. "Take a look, Red. I think we got 'em."

Hugh's glance shuttled to the barn, fifty feet away and to one side. He saw a moving shadow at the barn door, saw a man come out of it, and carefully walk the length of the wall until he suddenly cut out and ran directly across toward the wagon shed. From in back of the barn, at the far limits of the pasture, a gun cut loose in two quick bursts that sent puffs of dust striking up at the running man's heels.

Then he was in the shelter of the wagon shed and that far gun broke off its firing. The silence was heavy-laden.

Hugh watched the shadow of Red's legs cross before the opening where he lay. Then the man was fumbling with the hasp at the door, pulling it open.

Red took two steps inside, stood listening against the ominous silence. Then Hugh said softly: "I've got a gun on you, Red!"

The lighter shade of the ground through the open doorway outlined Red's suddenly stiffening frame. He whirled around, blurring up his gun in a sudden, beating explosion of sound. Hugh pressed the trigger of his gun, sure of his aim, and Red's stocky form jerked, and he gave a low moan and slowly toppled forward on his face. Hugh was on him a second later, wrenching the guns from his already lifeless hands.

Hugh threw himself face down in the dirt as the rifles at the house blazed alive once more, drowning out the echoes of the suddenly renewed firing from the posse's guns. He crawled back to the opening and lay there, looking out once more.

Then, unexpectedly, some marksman in the barn began systemically throwing his shots at the base of the shed's front wall, working outward from the door. Hugh heard the bullets splitting the rough board siding and came to his knees with a momentary panic coursing through him. Suddenly a bullet whipped into him, low on his left side, and he half spun about before he lost his footing and lay there on the floor, breathing heavily. For one tense minute he waited, half paralyzed, expecting a second bullet to reach him each instant.

When it didn't come, he crawled back to the opening and scanned the yard once again. He was barely in time, for a man's outline showed almost directly before him running for the door of the shed. Hugh nosed out the rifle at an angle and fired one shot, and the man's leaping run became an ungainly, forward sprawl.

They saw the powder flame of his gun, and now, an instant after he moved away, a dozen bullets searched out the opening and shredded the wood in the boards alongside. Hugh darted across the doorway to the other side of the building and pushed loose another board there, shoulder-high, so that it gave him a six-inch-wide opening to look through. Time and again he thanked those marksmen on the hill who seemed to have sensed what was going on down here and were keeping Keyes bottled in the house and barn.

"Hugh! Hugh, are you there?" Fay called, hysteria edging her voice.

"Still here."

The next moment he was listening to the sound of running horses coming in from the south from the direction of the Bull Forks trail. That would be Walt Andrews and George Baird and the rest, and a wild surge of hope leaped alive in him.

Then, above the beat of those faraway pounding hoofs, Hugh suddenly heard the crunching of boot soles on the gravel outside. A split second later, as he turned to face the door, a man's shadowy bulk loomed in the opening.

Some instinct guided that man's first blasting shot. As it momentarily lighted the shed's interior, Hugh saw another figure behind the first one, saw the twisted, expectant expression on the face of the man who had fired. Hugh felt his bullet gouge a searing concussion that drove the first man backward through the opening in a falling lunge. The man behind dodged his companion's hurtling bulk and lunged in through the opening and to one side of the door.

70

Moving out of his first position, Hugh didn't dare trust himself to a shot, knowing that he might miss and expose his own hiding place. The gun thunder outside, now beating to a higher pitch, drowned out all the small noises that might have given him a clue as to where the man stood. Cries and shouts up at the house told of the posse's arrival.

"I came down after you, Conner," a voice spoke out from across the shed. Even though the tone of that voice was muted by the explosions outside, Hugh recognized it as Keyes's. A stubborn pride and the knowledge that he had failed had brought Wyatt Keyes down here to hunt down the man who had ruined him. He could have ridden away without this last gesture, but he was choosing this way, instead. Grudgingly Hugh felt a small admiration for the man.

"Where are you, Conner?" Keyes called out in an interval when the guns outside were momentarily stilled.

When Hugh didn't answer, Fay Baird choked back a sob that was barely audible in the stillness.

"So the girl's alive, too." Keyes's voice already came from another position.

Hugh's eyes were searching the darkness at the front wall, in the direction from which Keyes's voice had sounded. His glance settled on the opening where he had torn loose the rotten board a few minutes ago. Through that long, rectangular opening showed a faint smear that was a patch of the lighter ground outside. Suddenly he saw a shadow blot out that faint blur of light, and in that split second he was arcing his gun into line.

He thumbed two shots at a point three feet above the opening, and, even as the light of the second blasting shot died out, he saw that he had failed, had given away his own position. For that burst of powder flame had showed him Keyes, standing to the other side of the opening, his square face set in a shrewd smile. He had purposely thrust his foot out over it, standing well to one side.

Hugh lunged out of position once more, but as he moved, Keyes's two guns blasted out an inferno of sound. Hugh went down under a crushing blow high up at his right shoulder, and from his knees he instinctively aimed at those gunfire flashes and worked the hammers of his six-guns.

A faintness hit him so that it was hard to swing the weapons down as they bucked in his hands. Time and time again he blasted shots at those orange winks of gun flame, until at last his hammers clicked metallically on empty chambers.

He tried to get to his feet, but lacked the strength. So he sat there, knowing that he made a perfect target, waiting for the bullets to whip into him.

Outside, men were shouting, and horses crossed the hard-packed yard at a wild run. The sharp explosions of the rifles gave way to the deeper throb of six-guns. A door swung shut at the barn, and a few moments later the yard was lit by the orange glow of flames. Someone had fired the barn.

Suddenly a figure was outlined in the doorway, and, as Hugh tried vainly to lift an empty Colt to cover the newcomer, a match flared alight, and Walt Andrews was standing there, looking down at him. The sheriff stepped back into the doorway and shouted: "Here they are, George! Bring a lantern!"

A minute later, when George Baird, a smoking gun in his fist, stood looking at Fay and Hugh, Andrews called across from the far side of the shed: "Here's where I sign my first death certificate, George."

Baird looked across and saw Wyatt Keyes's burly form lying awkwardly across a broken, upended keg. But what interested him most was that his daughter was in Hugh Conner's arms, her head against his chest.

Andrews saw it, too, and came over to stand behind his friend. Abruptly the lawman said: "Fay, Doc Painter's up at the house. I reckon it's safe for you to run up and get him. Hugh will need some fixin'."

When she had gone out the door, Andrews reached into his pocket and took out the telegram he had received that morning and handed it to Hugh. What it said was:

DON'T BOTHER TO ARREST HUGH CONNER. WITNESSES CLAIM SELF-DEFENSE. SORRY NO REWARD.

73

Death Brings in the Ophir

Jonathan Glidden completed the story he titled "Death Brings in the Ophir," in early August, 1938. It was submitted to Newsstand Publications, Inc., by his agent and was purchased on January 9, 1939. The author was paid $67.50. The title was changed to "A Gun-Boss for Eternal Range" when it appeared in *Complete Western Book Magazine* (5/39). It was subsequently reprinted in another magazine owned by the successor company to Newsstand Publications, appearing as "Bullet-Boss for Eternal Range" in *Best Western* (11/53). The text for its first appearance in book form is taken from the author's original typescript and the original title has been restored.

I

Circuit Judge Byron Morgan let his grizzled visage assume an expression of cold gravity as he looked down at the tall man standing before the bench.

"This injunction is granted," he stated firmly. "Mister Treacher, you will close down the Ophir Mine until such time as you have complied with the regulations set up by the county commissioners."

The sharp planes of Nick Treacher's thin face shaped a bleak smile, and he drawled: "Judge Morgan, the regulations and the county commissioners can go to hell."

On the heel of his words, several things happened at once. Sheriff Abe Stoops lifted his ponderous bulk from a chair flanking the high rostrum, muttering something unintelligible in his anger. Judge Morgan banged on his desk with his gavel against the sudden commotion from the spectators. A mixture of reactions held the thin crowd in the chairs back along the length of the room. There were a few stifled laughs. One or two men cursed loudly, and a thick-built man sitting alongside a girl in the front row of chairs came to his feet, yelling: "Your Honor, that's contempt of court! I demand that this man be arrested!"

Nick Treacher, as this man spoke, faced around in a deceptively slow-looking move. "Sure it's contempt, Sam. But not contempt of court. This stopped being a law court when you got to the commissioners with your bribe money."

Sam Poole's square face paled a shade. His flashing gray eyes didn't meet Nick Treacher's agate-colored ones as he barked: "As representative of the minority stockholders of the Ophir Mine, Your Honor, I demand this man's immediate arrest."

Judge Morgan's face was drawn in a look of cold fury, yet at Sam Poole's remark he was unsurprised. He regarded Treacher levelly for the space of two brief seconds, then said to Abe Stoops: "Sheriff, do your duty."

Stoops scowled, let his hand stray toward the butt of a .38 he wore in a holster at his fat thigh, and took two steps toward Treacher. Then something pulled him up as though he'd stepped against an invisible stone wall.

Nick Treacher, as the sheriff moved toward him, brushed back his coat in a smooth unbroken gesture. Lazily, yet smoothly, his hand palmed an ivory-handled Colt .45 from an open holster he wore, tied low at his right thigh. The weapon rocked out, settled in line with Stoops's sloping paunch.

"I was hopin' it wouldn't come to this," he said, stepping back to lean against a waist-high open window to one side of the bench, so that his glance commanded every occupant of the room. "But now that it has, you'll all understand this. The Ophir stays open. Any man who comes up there to serve a warrant on me or any of my men is likely to find it unhealthy." Lithely, with an ease good to see in a tall man, Nick Treacher put one hand on the sill of the window and vaulted through the opening.

As Treacher's high-built frame dropped out of sight, Sam Poole moved from his chair toward the window, his hand stabbing in under the lapel of his frock coat and coming out from a shoulder holster fisting a short-barreled six-gun. But at the exact instant he stepped to the opening to look down into the courtyard, an explosion ripped away the drowsy silence out there, and a splinter of wood flicked from the window frame squarely into Poole's face. It cut a long, jagged scratch down one cheek, bringing blood. Poole moved quickly out of the line of fire.

Sheriff Stoops lumbered heavily down the aisle between the rows of chairs and out the doors at the rear of the room, gun in hand. Sam Poole, blotting the blood from his cheek with a handkerchief, turned to the judge and said flatly: "I'll swear out the warrant."

The girl in the chair alongside the one Poole had occupied spoke for the first time: "Dad, you'll pull this whole thing down on your own head." There was more of pleading to her tone than of warning.

Her words brought the hint of a flush to Judge Morgan's face. He knocked on his oak-topped desk with his gavel, and his deep voice intoned: "Bailiff, clear the court immediately!"

While the bailiff quickly ushered out the small group of onlookers, Judge Morgan shifted nervously in his chair with his glance avoiding his daughter's.

Once the doors at the room's far end had swung shut, the judge eyed the girl severely and said: "Mary, I'll ask you to leave, too. There was no call for that remark of yours. I'm a judge even though I'm your father, and you'll show me the proper respect."

A look of tenderness came immediately to Mary Morgan's brown eyes as she regarded her parent. That look made the smooth, olive-hued oval of her face truly beautiful. It was a face much like her father's, aquiline yet lacking any sharp angularity, strong without the severe line of his blunt jaw. Her hair, a lustrous brown, exactly matched that dark hair that flecked the gray of the judge's shaggy head.

Mary met the reproof humbly: "I just want you to be sure you know what you're doing, Dad. Nick Treacher could be a dangerous man."

"The law knows how to deal with men like Treacher," Sam Poole put in. He walked over to the girl, took her arm with a proprietary gesture, and led her back to the doors. Then, when she had gone out, he faced the bench once more: "Your Honor, I don't want any mistake about this. Treacher must be behind bars within an hour, or I'll use my own methods."

"Careful, Poole," Judge Morgan cautioned with a show of stubbornness. "This is a court of law."

At the far corner of the open square around the courthouse, Nick Treacher swung into the saddle of a long-barreled bay horse at the hitch rail and spoke tersely to the man alongside: "We'd better make it fast, Ed. The sheriff just came down off the courthouse steps."

As Ed Wright reined his sorrel out into the thin traffic of the dusty street, he queried: "Trouble?"

"Plenty."

These two were outwardly as unalike as any two men could be. Nick Treacher's flat frame topped six feet by a good two inches, while Ed Wright's thick-set one lacked a good four inches of that mark. Treacher wore boots, a black broadcloth suit over a white shirt and string-tie, and a high-crowned, gray Stetson. Wright's outfit was a 'puncher's faded Levi's, cotton shirt, vest, flat-brimmed Stetson. Treacher spoke in a soft Texas drawl, Wright in the hard nasal twang of a Montana man. In these ways they were different.

Yet they were as fundamentally alike as the matched pair of Colts sagging from the worn holsters at Ed Wright's thighs. Each man had seen his share of trouble. Both pairs of eyes—Nick's a pure agate, Ed's a slate blue—could assume the same granite-like quality of hardness, and both had trained hand to gun in a precision that never failed. Both were sparing of words, unless in the company of friends—and both could count their real friends on the fingers of one hand.

As they took the first turning into a side street beyond the square, their ponies at a quick trot, Ed queried: "How bad is it?" He had ridden in from the north only four hours ago, barely in time to come down here from the Ophir with Nick and wait out the court hearing and understanding only a few of the more important details of what was happening.

"Last night the county commissioners passed an ordinance closing down any mine operating in the county employing less than forty men."

Ed's thin brows came up knowingly. "And your outfit works only fifteen. What the hell kind of a ruling is that?"

Nick Treacher laughed mirthlessly. "One intended to crowd us out. They're within their rights, of course. But the commissioners are a mangy lot, and their palms are sticky."

"Meanin' that this gent Poole gave them some money to grab onto?"

Nick shrugged his wide shoulders. "It's only a guess."

They reached the far limits of the street, started up a steeply climbing slope that led upward the half mile to the lip of the rim. Along the face of the slope, far above, the shaft houses and fan-spread scars of muck dumps showed the locations of half a dozen mines. Smoke came from the chimneys of only two of the shaft houses, showing as clearly as the nearly deserted streets of the town that the days of the boom were past, that in another ten years Strike would be played out, forgotten along with half a hundred other ghost camps.

Ed said: "Maybe you ought to begin at the beginnin' and tell me about it. First, why did you pick a camp like this, instead of one that's boomin'? Or is it any of my business?"

"I made it your business when I wrote asking you to come down here," Nick told him. He knew Ed as well as he'd ever known any man. Further, he trusted him. So there was no reserve as he went on: "I'm workin' a different line this time. The town's folded up. People pullin' out every day. A year ago, when I came here, it was just beginnin' to hit the downgrade. I looked it over, found the Ophir shut down because the ledge they were workin' had shallowed out. It was plain luck that I took a closer look at the ledge. From then on I knew that it was the Ophir I wanted."

"How come?" Ed was plainly puzzled.

"A hunch, Ed. I don't think the Ophir's played out. Good men haven't paid much attention to this field . . . not with Tombstone and Bisbee boomin' the way they are."

"So you took out an option?"

Nick nodded. "Every cent I have to my name is in the option and the payroll to cover this three-months' operation. I still have thirty days to go. At the end of my option, I must show production of at least seven hundred ounces of silver."

"Show it to whom?"

"The men who will buy the Ophir put up the money to open it wide. My hunch is that we'll run into a bigger pocket than the one that started this rush. But that'll come later, maybe a year from now. The main thing now is to prove out under this option. Once that's done, the buyers are naming me superintendent and manager and giving me a third of their stock issue."

"It listens good," Ed admitted. "But why bring me in on it?"

"Because I want to see you runnin' your own brand up in Montana by this time next year."

Ed's glance whipped around to meet Nick's. "Say that again."

"It's up to you, Ed. From now on it's the Ophir against the law. If you'll throw in with me, we'll take a long shot. Your share will be half of anything I get out of this as long as you live."

Ed swallowed with difficulty. "Me, a millionaire?"

"Maybe . . . if you miss gettin' fitted with a wooden nightshirt first.'

"Hell, that don't matter!" Ed was remembering a time, four years ago, when Nick Treacher's bullet had cut down a drunken glory hunter over in Santa Fé and saved his life. That had been their first meeting, the beginning of a real friendship. "I'm in this, Nick, no matter which way your luck goes. Now what about this gent, Poole?"

"He saw the same thing I did, that the Ophir wasn't played out. Only he turned up after I'd taken out the option, so he's corralled enough of the old stock-holders to give him a legal right to act as their representative. Now he's trying to stop me from proving on my option. He has money behind him, lots of it."

"But you claimed this mornin' that this Judge Morgan was square."

Nick's brows gathered in a worried frown. "That's the only thing that doesn't fit. Morgan is square. Ordinarily he wouldn't make this kind of a play." It was only Nick's instinct that told him this, plus the remembrance of the girl, Mary Morgan, who had sat, tight-lipped and silent, throughout the hearing. To him, this girl had the same stamp of the Thoroughbred as her father. He honestly admitted that the two or three times he'd met and spoken to her on the streets of the town had given him more respect and liking for her than for any woman he could remember, and for the father he held the same respect.

"So what do we do now?" Ed queried.

Nick turned in the saddle, pointed back along the trail. Down there, now hitting the foot of the abrupt slope, a rider was pushing a horse up toward them. The rider's shape was big enough to dwarf that of his pony. "That'll be Abe Stoops. Likely as not he's got a warrant to serve on me."

"You goin' to let him?"

"What do you think?"

Nick's answer brought a wide smile to Ed Wright's sun-blackened face. They spurred their ponies into a stiffer trot and in ten more minutes were climbing onto the bench and through the gate in the high board fence that enclosed the gray-painted shaft house of the Ophir.

Inside the enclosure, climbing out of his saddle at the hitch rail in front of the small office, Nick Treacher reached down and lifted his single weapon an inch from its holster, letting it slip back again. "You can get Tom Baker to let you down into the shaft in the skip, Ed. He'll stop you at the level the gang's workin' today. Bring 'em back up with you. I want them to see this."

"You sure you can handle this badge-toter?"

Nick smiled, and Ed disappeared into the open maw of the shaft house door. As Nick listened to the first faint hoof thuds of Sheriff Abe Stoops's climbing pony outside the fence, the gears of the winch in the shaft house rattled to announce that the skip was on its way down into the main shaft.

Outside the gate a moment later, Stoops called in a loud voice: "Open up, Treacher!"

Nick walked over to the gate, threw it open. Stoops sat his saddle less than ten feet beyond, a six-gun clenched in his ham-like fist, his thick lips curled down in a leering smile. His weapon was aimed squarely at Nick.

"I don't want no trouble from you, Treacher," Stoops drawled. "Stick up your mitts and walk out here. You're under arrest."

Nick laughed softly. Without turning, he called loudly—"Watch him, Ed!"—and added in a normal voice: "I've got a man up in the cupola with a Winchester lined at your belt buckle, Stoops. Unless you want your guts spilled all over the side of this hill, you'll leather that cutter and climb down and walk in here."

Abe Stoops hand faltered, fell away, and his glance whipped upward to the cupola atop the shaft house. It was an open-timbered box, housing the pulley for the skip cable coming from the winch, the sky behind it outlining every detail. The lawman looked hard, didn't see what he had thought he would.

As his glance came down to Nick Treacher again, he saw his mistake all at once, the mistake any man would have made in taking his eyes off Treacher for one split second. Treacher stood in the same position, with the same smile, except that now the ivory-butted six-gun rested surely in his palm, lined rock-steady at Stoops. The lawman's own weapon had shifted four inches out of line. It might as well have been in a bureau drawer in Stoops's house down in town.

"You're softer than you look, Abe, which is sayin' plenty," Nick drawled. "Are you goin' to make a try for me, or will you throw up your hands and ride that lug head in here and pay us a call?"

The ruddy tan of Abe Stoops's loosely jowled face

had gone a sickly yellow. For a brief moment his quick-raising anger made him hesitate, calculating his chances. But even in that anger he saw that there wasn't a chance, and with a muttered unintelligible oath he let his weapon fall from his grasp, raised his hands above his head, and rode in through the gate.

Ten minutes later, Ed Wright emerged from the shaft house door leading a group of twelve men whose grimy faces and soiled bib overalls announced them for what they were: the Ophir's mine crew. They were a hard-bitten lot, mostly Irish and Swedes.

Ed must have partly prepared them for what they would see, for when they glimpsed Abe Stoops, standing with arms upraised before the hitch rail alongside his pony, every man among them laughed.

One Irishman called—"Get a pair o' sky-hooks to hang onto, Abe!"—and that brought a louder burst of harsh laughter.

Stoops was in need of sky-hooks. From the fine perspiration that beaded his forehead and the flushed look to his face, it was obvious that the effort of keeping his arms over his head was fast becoming painful. Strangely enough, he was holding this posture even though Nick's .45 was in its holster. He was plainly a thoroughly cowed man.

Suddenly reaching the limit of his patience, Stoops lowered his arms, growled: "Get it over with!"

This gesture of defiance brought another laugh from the crew, although Nick immediately gestured them to silence. The fact that they obeyed that gesture showed a measure of the respect they held for him.

Three months ago, at the first hint of Sam Poole's belligerence, Nick had realized the need for a tough crew in the event of trouble. He had spent a good share of his money gathering these men from the boom camps he knew, paying them enough to insure their loyalty, picking the fighters. Each man knew him, knew of his reputation as a shrewd mine oper-ator, and now the fact that they clearly sided with him against this representative of the law was the last thing he needed to settle the thing he had in mind.

"Stoops came up here to arrest me," he announced. "Do you think I ought to go back to town with him?"

A mutter of protest greeted his words, one that wiped out the lawman's paleness and put in its place an angry flush of color.

"The county commissioners claim they'll close down the Ophir unless I hire a crew of forty men," Nick went on. "I can't afford that with money out of my own pocket. But supposin' we keep the sheriff up here until the town or the country commissioners pay us five thousand dollars for his release? With that five thousand I can hire the twenty-five men I need to meet the commissioners' ordinance. How does it sound, gents?"

For a moment a tense silence held the group as the idea took hold. All at once a roar of shouted approval welled from the throats of the mine crew.

"Ed!" Nick called above the clamor of voices. "Get

me a sheet of paper and a pencil out of the office. The rest of you get on below and to work. All but two . . . O'Reilly and Jensen. You two can get rifles out of the office and climb up into the cupola and keep a watch on the trail."

Less than a quarter hour later Abe Stoops, standing in the hard-packed rectangle of ground before the office, said to Nick: "You ain't got the guts to back this play, Treacher."

For his answer, Nick pointed to the gate and to the cupola above the shaft house. Ed Wright was on his way through the gate with a sheet of paper in his pocket, a notice that was to be tacked to an awning post in front of Strike's biggest saloon. In the pulley cage on the sloping roof of the shaft house, the shapes of Tim O'Reilly and Nels Jensen showed against the patchwork of the timber. Looking up there, seeing the Winchesters cradled across the knees of those two men, Stoops swallowed with difficulty.

One minute later he was locked in the Ophir's tool house.

II

Ed Wright, a stranger to Strike, decided to go a little beyond the instructions he'd received from Nick Treacher. It was early afternoon and the streets of the town were nearly empty under the heat of a scorching Arizona sun. Ed came out of the saddle at the partly filled hitch rail in front of the Pay Dirt Saloon, listlessly threw his sorrel's reins over the tie bar, and sauntered over onto the awninged walk.

He picked an awning post with a shoulder-high nail in it to lean against. He stood there for almost three minutes, long enough to take out a sack of Durham and build a smoke and light it, to scan lazily the courthouse square opposite, and to reach inconspicuously behind him and scratch between his shoulder blades. Had there been a close observer, he would have noticed that Ed's scratching was a little awkward. For when Ed finally sauntered across the plank walk and through the swing doors of the Pay Dirt, a white sheet of paper hung from the nail that had prodded him between the shoulder blades.

Ed had half finished his glass of beer at the bar when he heard the shout on the street outside. He was as curious as the other half dozen occupants of the saloon, all of whom sauntered up front as the shout rang out a second time.

A man burst in through the door, waving the sheet of paper in his hand, shouting: "Goddlemighty, get this, gents! Abe Stoops bein' held for ransom!"

The bartender snatched the paper from him and read aloud: "This is to notify any interested party that Abel Stoops, sheriff of Río Arriba County, today climbed the hill to the Ophir Mine to arrest Nick Treacher. The trip left the sheriff exhausted. He claims he won't come down again for love or money . . . at least not for any less than five thousand dollars." The barkeeper added: "It's signed by Nick Treacher."

At least two listeners, Ed Wright noticed, looked as though they wanted to laugh. But they didn't, and in this willful restraint, along with the bartender's dry comment—"Sam Poole's goin' to love this!"—Ed had his first insight into the power Sam Poole's money commanded in this dying town. It was obvious that these men feared Poole, that he commanded a belligerent respect in them.

"You take it across to his office, Ben," the bartender said.

"Not me!" a bearded oldster retorted. "He's your boss, not mine."

Ed turned to the man nearest, queried blandly and in a loud voice: "Who's this Sam Poole?"

"You don't know Sam Poole?" The man was incredulous. He turned to the bartender, grinned maliciously: "This gent doesn't know who Sam Poole is."

The barkeeper looked sharply at Ed. "Stranger in town?" he queried. Then, catching Ed's nod, he let his glance travel downward, to the twin holsters at Ed's thighs. He queried abruptly: "Lookin' for work?"

Ed said: "That depends."

"Sam Poole's got jobs to hand out," the barkeep went on. He held out the sheet of paper. "You might take this over to him and ask him for work at the same time. Second door to the right in the hallway above the Miner's Bank."

Ed took the paper, said—"Thanks, mister."—and went out through the swing doors. Outside the Pay

Dirt, he hesitated long enough to catch the subdued laughter of the men he had left in there. Then he went on.

On the second right-hand doorway in the hall above the bank, Ed read the lettering on the frosted glass panel:

SAMUEL POOLE
CONSULTANT ON MINING
OPHIR DEVELOPMENT COMPANY

He knocked, opened the door before he got his answer, and stepped into a room to find two men uneasily looking toward the door. He immediately decided that the one sitting in the swivel chair behind the ornately carved pine desk, the one with the thick heavy shoulders, barrel chest, and blunt visage, was Sam Poole. The other, older, with a shaggy head of gray hair flecked with brown, honest-looking brown eyes, and a wide longhorn mustache sat in a chair on one side wall facing the desk. It was Judge Morgan.

Poole rapped out irritably: "Men don't walk in here. . . ."

"Lay off the talk," Ed cut in, his blue eyes gone cold and inscrutable. "You're Poole?"

Sam Poole, for the moment speechless at this arrogance, nodded.

Ed came over to the desk, tossed the sheet of paper on it, and said: "No one over at the saloon had the guts to bring this up here." As Poole picked up the paper and hastily scanned the lines, Ed took out the makings and built a smoke.

Five seconds later Poole's chair pounded backward into the wall as its occupant lunged to his feet. Poole cursed viciously, glared at Ed: "Where'd you get this? You know this Treacher?" His look was hard, menacing.

Ed said evenly: "Who's Treacher? I came up here after a job."

The calmness of his answer changed Poole's belligerent attitude to a calculating one. For the first time he looked carefully at this stranger, seeing the same thing that had attracted the barkeeper's attention less than five minutes ago. All at once he handed the sheet of paper across to Judge Morgan, waiting until the judge had finished reading before he said: "We can use this man."

Morgan's face had paled a little. "Better think twice before you do anything," he warned.

"I'll handle this, Morgan," Poole said sharply. Then to Ed: "Can you use that pair of cutters, stranger?"

"If I couldn't, I wouldn't be luggin' 'em around."

"You're after work? What kind?"

"Anything you call work that ain't."

Poole reached over and pulled a vacant chair closer to the desk. He was smiling thinly when he said: "Have a seat, friend."

"This'll do," was Ed's rejoinder. He stood where he was.

"Would you take five hundred dollars for a night's work?" Poole asked abruptly, bluntly.

Ed's brows came up. His answer was equally as blunt: "That sounds like killer's money. If it is, make it a thousand."

Poole frowned. "You aren't known here?"

"I wouldn't be here if I was."

"It's a deal. Sit down and we'll talk it over."

As Ed finally took the chair, Judge Morgan rose, his look plainly uncomfortable. "I'll be going back to the office, Sam," he said nervously.

Poole laughed mirthlessly: "No, you don't, Morgan. We're in this together, and damned if you can crawl out of it now."

Morgan sighed weakly, letting himself down into the chair once again without protest.

An hour before dark, Tim O'Reilly shouted down from the cupola of the Ophir shaft house to Nick Treacher: "Someone's comin' up the trail."

Nick made his way across the darkened enclosure to the gate, opening it a scarce four inches so that he could scan the pale ribbon of the hill trail. Soon he made out the figure of a rider. When the rider was close enough so that Nick could catch the lines of his pony, the gate opened wider, and Nick stepped out.

"You took your time," he said to Ed, as the sorrel came to a stop under a tight rein.

"I needed time," Ed told him, as he swung out of the saddle. He let out a gusty sigh and added: "I've seen a few forked *hombres* in my time, but none like this Poole."

"You saw Poole?"

"Better than that. I'm workin' for him." He reached into this pocket, pulling out a thick roll of paper money. "Here's five hundred. I'm to get five hundred more as soon as I've put a bullet into you.

Nick smiled. "Nice work," he said. But his smile disappeared as he caught Ed's sober look. "What happened?"

"I don't like it, Nick. Poole isn't interested in gettin' his sheriff out of here. All he wants is either to toll you down to town so's he can work on you, or to have me arrange for your funeral. He said it didn't matter much. I could either bring you back with me or put a slug in you up here. He talks like he meant it."

"That's no news. What're you worried about?"

"If I don't come through for him, he can hire plenty others who'll make the try. Nick, you be careful."

For a long moment Nick Treacher was silent. Then he said: "Let's get out of sight." Then, once the gate was closed and barred behind them, he asked quickly: "You're sure Poole doesn't know who you are?"

Ed shook his head. "I'm a stranger from out of the country. I don't know Nick Treacher. I didn't even know Sam Poole or Morgan."

"You saw Morgan?"

"He was in Poole's office. Wanted to leave when Poole started making his deal with me. Only Poole wouldn't let him."

Nick stared thoughtfully at Ed in deliberation, then abruptly he turned and called softly—"O'Reilly."—

and waited until a man's shape came out of the cobalt shadow alongside the shaft house. "Tim, can you and Jensen and a couple more hold this place until we get back?"

"We've got the sheriff, Nick," Tim answered.

"That may not mean so much," Nick told him. "It seems they don't think much of the sheriff down below. You may have to use your guns."

"Then we'll use 'em, Nick." Tim O'Reilly was positive about that.

"We may be gone all night," Nick said. "Rout out two more of the boys and keep a sharp watch. Don't shoot unless you have to."

O'Reilly disappeared once more into the shadow of the shaft house.

Ed asked worriedly: "Now what have you got in your craw?"

Nick reached up and took a hold on the left sleeve of his coat, rolling it up. He took off his Stetson, crumpled it out of shape, mussed his hair, and rubbed more dust into it. He scratched the length of his left forearm with a broken stick of wood he found on the ground nearby. Blood ran from the welts along his arm.

Ed watched at first in puzzlement, then in impatience. Finally, when Nick reached over and lifted one of Ed's six-guns from his holster and fired two shots into the air, Ed said in thinly veiled sarcasm: "Don't tell me, friend!"

"You're takin' me into Poole." Nick dropped Ed's .45 back into the leather.

"Are you loco?"

"Poole trusts you. You can get away any time you want. This is the only way to force his hand, Ed."

"His hand don't need forcin'. We know all there is to know."

"Everything but how he tolled Morgan in on this. I tell you, Morgan's honest. If we can find out what hold Poole has on him, we can bust this wide open."

"I won't do it, Nick."

"Why not? If Poole's got me where he wants me, he may talk."

Ed hesitated.

Nick pressed his point. "All you'll have to do is bring me an iron and the two of us can get clear of any trouble Sam Poole can make."

Reluctantly Ed said: "All right, we'll give it a try. But I still don't like it."

Two minutes later they were on their way down the hill trail. Halfway down, Ed said: "Ride in close to me a second, Nick."

Nick, puzzled, reined his bay in alongside Ed's sorrel. Then, before Nick could dodge, Ed had whipped a six-gun from holster and brought it slashing down on Nick's skull. It was a hard blow, making the lights of the town below dance before Nick's eyes. It hurt, yet the unsteadiness of Nick's senses lasted for only a few seconds. He reined out of reach, smiling wryly against the pain: "I hadn't thought of that. It'll make it look better." Reaching a hand up, he could feel his hair a sticky mass over the spot where Ed's gun barrel had connected.

Entering the main street, where the lights of the store windows washed out feebly across the planks of the awninged walks, Ed drew a six-gun and lined it at Nick, who rode ahead. In front of the Pay Dirt Ed snapped: "Hold it, Treacher!" Then more loudly, he called: "Someone tell Poole he's got a caller out here!"

Three loungers along the walk had been watching the two riders for the last quarter minute. Suddenly one of them stared intently at Nick and breathed— "Hell, he's brought Treacher in."—and turned and ran in through the swing doors.

Shouts issued from the opening in the front of the saloon. A scuffle of boots sounded from inside, and a moment later the doors burst outward from Sam Poole's thick-set bulk. He came to the edge of the walk, standing there spraddle-legged.

"Nice work, stranger," he said to Ed. His square-jawed face took on a half sneer as he intently regarded Nick Treacher. He saw the torn clothes, the mussed hair, the smeared face; last of all, he must have seen the trickle of blood that etched a thin line down one side of Nick's face from the cut above his ear. Suddenly he laughed and said: "We heard the shots a few minutes ago. You let a two-bit gunslinger clean house on you, Treacher? Hell, I thought you were tough!"

"It may look like two bits to you, Poole, but it's five hundred on the line now, or I take him back where he came from." Ed spoke flatly, his voice not raised, carrying the sham of his identity.

Poole didn't argue. He reached into a coat pocket, lifted out a wallet, and calmly thumbed out five one-hundred-dollar bills. Stepping out to hand them up to Ed, he said with a touch of admiration in his voice: "I didn't think I'd ever have to pay this. Stick around, stranger. I can use you." Then, wheeling about, he called to two men in the small crowd now standing on the walk: "Curly, you and Mike take Treacher to the jail. Luke, get on up to Morgan's place and tell him he's wanted down here."

Five minutes later, at the jail, Sam Poole stepped in behind Curly and Mike, who were leading Nick Treacher to the open door of one of the four cells. "Turn him around, boys," he said.

Then, as Mike and Curly each held one of Nick's arms, Poole drew back his fist and swung a full blow squarely into Nick's face. Held as he was, all Nick could do was move his head. It didn't help. Poole's slamming fist struck him alongside the jaw. His head fell weakly to one side, and his knees gave way.

Ed, who had followed Poole to the jail, spoke from the doorway: "You believe in holdin' all the aces, don't you?"

"And what if I do?" Sam Poole queried, turning on this hired stranger.

Ed shrugged. "Nothin'. Only he's goin' to remember that."

Poole smiled, his quick belligerence fading. "He won't have much longer to remember anything."

Ed's brows came up. "It could be arranged," he admitted. "For, say, another thousand?"

Poole deliberated a moment. "Not a bad idea," he admitted at length. "Not bad at all. Play along with me, stranger, and you'll leave here well-heeled."

At almost the exact moment Poole took Ed's arm and walked back through the sheriff's office, Sheriff Abe Stoops was wiping the perspiration from his bald head in the Ophir tool house. Stoops had worked more in the past hour than ever in his life. With a crowbar he had found on one of the work benches, he'd succeeded in prying a board of sheathing loose from one of the two-by-four uprights of the tool house's back wall. Because of his bulk, it had been necessary to waste fifteen more minutes prying loose a second.

Now, as he pushed the boards out and scanned the darkness outside, he wasn't so sure. The muscles along his back crawled as he remembered his several glimpses of the stolid-faced Irishmen he'd seen pacing the lighted, hard-packed yard before the shaft house a few minutes ago. Those Irishmen had been carrying rifles, and Abe Stoops didn't relish the possibility of one of those Winchesters being lined at him.

Nevertheless, he knew Sam Poole well enough to realize that Sam would be through with him for this prime blunder unless he got down to town tonight. When Sam Poole was finished with a man, that man's future was as clearly patterned as a prisoner's serving life sentence inside Yuma prison. Sam Poole was already the political boss of Strike. Without his good will, no lawman could last in the town.

So Abe made his choice, squeezing out through the still narrow opening, running as noiselessly as he could to the fence twenty yards away. He was thankful for the darkness. Going over the fence he tore his trousers and shirt and ripped the palms of his hands open on the strand of barbwire topping the fence. Yet once outside, hearing no exploding shot behind him, Strike's sheriff breathed an intense sigh of relief.

III

Mary Morgan was positive about her answer to Luke Selden, the man Poole had sent after the judge. "Father's in bed, asleep, and I won't wake him."

"But Sam said for me to bring him along," Luke insisted.

"Sam Poole can wait." Mary gave Luke her best smile. "Dad's had a hard day. Now, please, don't make me get him up."

Luke was only human. The smiles of less pretty girls had before this softened him. Rather than offend this girl, who, after all, was being courted by Sam Poole, he'd go back and get further instructions. He even thought to tip his hat as he backed off the wide porch, saying: "I reckon you're right, miss. I'll tell Sam to wait until mornin'."

Mary, as she closed the door, wondered what new thing had happened to involve her father with Sam Poole. Today, at the court hearing, she'd seen Poole as he really was for the first time in these four months she'd known him. She'd seen all too clearly the power the man held over her father, and immediately a man she'd looked upon as a prospective husband—simply because her father had picked him—became as repulsive and dishonest as he had seemed kind and considerate before now.

This had been a hard day for her. Rather than go directly to her father and talk this out with him, she'd chosen to wait, to think the matter through for herself. Perhaps in contrast to her sudden insight into Poole's dishonesty had come as sudden a liking for Nick Treacher. She had known Treacher casually for nearly the same length of time that she had known Poole. He was a soft-spoken, quiet man, always courteous, never openly staring at her or intruding on his chance acquaintance as she remembered Sam Poole's doing. Treacher's sudden and impulsive move in the courtroom had startled her, for she had never once glimpsed the rashness that lay behind the quiet good-humor in his make-up. She knew that he had been in the right, that he would fight, and now she found herself siding with him against her father.

She had undressed and was in bed twenty minutes after Luke had gone, when abruptly she heard the tread of boots along the porch out front and then an insistent knocking at the door. She was about to get out of bed to put on her robe and answer the knock when she heard her father's door across the hall crack open on its hinges.

Judge Morgan went along the hall, across the living room, and the lock on the front door clicked. Then Mary heard a gruff voice say: "How come you didn't show up when Luke came after you?" It was Sam Poole who had spoken.

"Luke must have talked to Mary," was her father's answer. "I was asleep."

"Never mind," Poole said, as the door slammed shut. "Can we talk here? Can Mary hear us?"

"I'll close the door." The judge's step crossed the living room, and the door at the end of the hall closed softly.

Mary reached for the quilted robe thrown over the chair alongside the bed. She put it on as she went out her door, and along the hall to the doorway to the living room. She was in time to hear Poole say, his voice muted by the panel: "We've got Treacher in jail."

Her father's gasp of incredulity was clearly audible.

Then Poole went on: "That salty gent that came to my office this afternoon turned the trick. He went up alone and brought Treacher back with him. Treacher looks like he'd tangled with a pack o' bob-cats."

"What does it mean, Sam?"

"That Treacher's through."

"I won't stand for murder, Sam. I'll back you in anything else. But not murder!" Judge Morgan's tone was harsh, angry.

"Think again," boomed Sam Poole's voice. "Remember what happened up in Clovis twenty-four years ago."

Mary only partly understood Poole's meaning. Twenty-four years ago, before he'd come down here into Arizona to marry his wife, Byron Morgan had top-handed a big outfit up in Wyoming, near Clovis. He'd been vague about those years, for some reason hesitating in ever mentioning his work up there.

"Sam," said her father, "it's a coward's trick to keep holding that over my head."

"No matter what it is, I'll turn you in for that murder unless you play along with me, Morgan. Wouldn't it be nice if I was to collect that two thousand reward still standing for you?"

"It wasn't murder!" Judge Morgan flared. "It was self-defense. Fred Royer had his gun out before I went for mine. I beat him fairly."

"Prove it! There wasn't a witness."

Mary felt herself going faint. Here, then, was the thing Sam Poole had held over her father, the reason her father had lost his integrity as a judge along with his self-respect. It was hard to believe that her father had killed a man. Yet here it was, the admission coming from her father himself.

A long-drawn silence followed Sam Poole's accusing words. Finally Byron Morgan spoke again, his voice lower, lifeless: "You hold all the aces, Sam. Call the deal."

"That's more like it. Now, here's the way we'll

work it. Tonight this gent that went up after Treacher and brought him down stands guard at the jail. He's goin' to get careless. He's goin' to give Treacher the chance to break jail. Treacher will make the break once he has the chance. I'll put half a dozen men out for him, and we'll head for the Ophir. Tomorrow mornin', Curly Bates will be found dead just below the Ophir fence."

"More murder. This time it'll be on your head, Sam."

"Prove it." Sam laughed, echoing his insolence of a minute ago.

"You'd kill one of your own men just to frame Treacher with murder?"

"Why not? I'm out to get the Ophir. Two years from now I'll have a million dollars in my pocket. It's worth one understrapper to get that. Besides, Curly's gettin' big ideas. I'm through with him."

"Sam, you stink enough to make a polecat tuck his tail and run."

Once again Sam Poole's booming laughter echoed out through the room beyond the door. "Have it your own way, Judge. Only remember. You'll be the one to convict Nick Treacher of murder, to see him hanged legally."

Numbed by a paralysis of fear and loathing, Mary Morgan turned and ran back along the wall into her own room. Her frantic thoughts didn't take on any pattern of reason until five minutes later, when she heard the slamming of the front door.

She quickly lit the lamp on the washstand, and then opened her door as her father's steps came along the hallway outside. The light caught him squarely, showing clearly the grim set to his face.

He was startled, saying awkwardly: "I thought you were asleep."

"Come in, Dad. I want to talk to you."

He came through the door, his glance puzzled.

"Dad, I heard everything you and Sam Poole just said." She was calm in the face of her father's amazement and chagrin. "Now I want to hear the rest of it. What happened twenty-four years ago, and how did Sam Poole find out about it."

It hurt her to see the reaction her words brought in her father. In the five seconds he had listened to her, his weathered, rugged face had taken on added years, his shoulders had sagged, and he had the look of a beaten man.

"I . . . I'd give anything if you hadn't done that, Mary."

"Sooner or later I'd have known. Dad, I want to help." Her voice abruptly took on tenderness. "There must be something we can do."

He shook his head. "Sam has too strong a hold on me. I did kill a man long before I met your mother, before I settled down. It was a scrap over a cattle trade. This man, Royer, thought I'd cheated him out of some money. We met alone on a trail up near Clovis one day. He didn't say a word but went for his gun. He shot first, his bullet grazing my shoulder. Mine took him through the chest. When I saw what I'd done, I ran and rode the length of two states before I picked a place to live. It was here, and in two more years I'd married your mother."

"How did Sam Poole find out about it?"

"He worked that Wyoming country last year, before he came here. He met someone up there who told him about me, someone from Clovis. It was pure circumstance that I proved to be the Byron Morgan he'd heard about."

"Couldn't a man in your position, with your reputation for honesty, give himself up to the law with the hope of getting off?"

Judge Morgan shook his head. "Not now. Several months ago, maybe, but not now. I've done too many dishonest things for Sam Poole in a legal way. He paid me three thousand dollars . . . the county commissioners a thousand each . . . to put through that ruling that worked against Nick Treacher this morning. I'd kill him, only that he's left evidence against me with a lawyer who'll expose me the minute anything happens to him."

Mary sat on the edge of the bed, studying her father, his helplessness and defeat hurting like an open sore. But abruptly some inner thought brought her to her feet. She took her father's arm, pushing him gently toward the door. "Get some sleep," she told him. "I think I know a way out. I'll tell you about it tomorrow." She kissed him on the forehead and closed the door before he could question her. As soon as she heard his door close farther along the hall, she went swiftly to the wardrobe, took out a dress, put it on.

At the Pay Dirt's bar, Sam Poole and Luke Selden and Abe Stoops spent ten minutes in earnest talk. The sheriff was obviously tired and disgruntled, but with the look of a whipped dog he stubbornly gave his attention to Poole, knowing that his future as a lawman depended on it.

Finally Sam Poole tossed off the shot glass of whisky at his elbow and said to Luke: "You've got it?"

Luke nodded. "I'm to send that fake hardcase over here, and then give Treacher his chance."

"Make it smooth, Luke," Sam Poole cautioned. "Treacher's no fool. It'll have to look right. Get goin'."

Poole watched Luke go out through the swing doors, then turned to Abe Stoops, eyeing him intently. "Abe, maybe I ought to thank you for puttin' me square on this friend o' Treacher's. As it is, I haven't decided yet. Anyone who'd set foot in the trap you did today shouldn't be totin' a law badge, my law badge."

"Sam, it won't happen again. Give me another try at Treacher."

Poole laughed mockingly. "I'll keep you as far out of this as I can," he said. "Now isn't any time to use a man who makes mistakes. Go home and get some sleep." He turned his back on Stoops, who hung his head and trudged slowly out through the swing doors.

At the jail, alongside the courthouse, Luke was saying to Ed Wright: "The boss wants me to spell you tonight. He says to come over to the Pay Dirt and have a drink and then turn in. Big doin's tomorrow."

Ed was mildly surprised. "Such as?"

Luke shrugged. "You'll have to get it from the boss."

Ed got up out of the swivel chair behind the sheriff's scarred oak desk, stretched and yawned, and went to the door. "See you tomorrow," he said as he went out.

Two minutes later Luke unlocked the steel door to the jail, hung his keys from a shell in his twin belts, and went in carrying a lantern. Nick Treacher sat up on the cot in the end cell, blinking sleepily against the lantern's light.

"Just makin' sure you're still here," Luke explained. He set the lantern down, took a sack of tobacco from a shirt pocket, and leaned indolently back against the wall while he built a smoke. "The boss ain't sure but what that Irish crew of yours will try to break you out of here."

Nick got up off the cot and came to the cell door. "Where's your friend?" he queried. "The ranny that brought me in tonight?"

"Poundin' his ear in bed by this time."

Nick made a pretense of feeling in his coat and shirt pockets for tobacco. Luke caught the gesture, read it rightly. "Out of the makin's?" he queried. Then, as Nick nodded, he stepped over to the cell and handed

108

his sack of tobacco through. As Nick's long-fingered hands sifted the dusty tobacco onto the wheat-straw paper, Luke leaned idly against the cell door. The gun in the holster at his left thigh was within six inches of the bars.

Luke pretended not to notice Nick's quick glance down to his waist. To cover up his inattention, he said: "You don't stand a prayer, Treacher. Poole's goin' to get this over with in. . . ."

As Nick's hand flashed out through the bars, Luke made a futile lunge back out of the way, timing it purposely too late. Then, as his own gun swung up and lined squarely at him, he let the stub of the cigarette drop from between his thin lips and lifted his hands, saying hollowly: "Don't! Don't shoot! I'll do anything you say."

"Then make it fast gettin' this door open!" Nick drawled, drawing back the weapon's hammer.

Luke made it fast, his hand shaking. This was partly through fear, for no man who carries a hair-trigger .45 enjoys staring into the bore of his own cocked weapon.

As the door swung open, Nick stepped out. Luke was busy pulling the key from the lock when Nick suddenly swung the heavy Colt up and down in a tight arc that ended alongside Luke's skull.

He went down, his last conscious thought being that he wouldn't have agreed to do this job if he'd realized a gun whipping was involved.

Nick, warily entering the sheriff's office after dragging Luke inside the cell and locking it, saw his own ivory-handled Colt and holster and belt hanging from a peg above the sheriff's desk. He crossed the room, took down his weapon, and belted it on, throwing Luke's .45 into the wastebasket on the far side of the room.

His six-gun was in his hand as he went out the door. He was less than twenty feet out from the door, headed diagonally out across the heavily shaded courthouse yard, when a call stopped him: "Nick Treacher!"

His first impulse was to line the weapon in his hand in the direction of that voice. He made out a shape under the spreading deep shadow of a cottonwood and was about to call out when sudden memory of that voice came to him. He let his hand fall to his side and walked over there.

It was Mary Morgan. As he approached, her tall, graceful figure came out in clear detail, and once again, as many times before now, her look filled him with admiration.

"You must listen," she said quickly. "There may not be much time." And she told him what had happened that night, of her father's conversation with Sam Poole, of the plan to frame him with Curly Bates's murder. She omitted telling him only one thing: how it happened that her father was Sam Poole's accomplice.

When she had finished, Nick Treacher was silent for several seconds. Finally he put the question she dreaded yet knew was coming: "Haven't you for-gotten something?"

When she didn't answer, he went on: "If I knew the thing that had pulled your father into this, I'd be able to bust it wide open."

Mary Morgan made her decision then, firm in the knowledge that sooner or later she'd have to trust someone and wanted it to be this Nick Treacher, if it was anyone. She told Nick all she had heard that night, both from Poole and her father, of the shoot-out that had taken twenty-four years to become a threat to an honest man's existence.

Ending, she said: "So you see we're all helpless before Sam Poole. He can beat you with the law simply because he's bought the law through black-mail."

"He's no proof against bullets."

"No, you couldn't do that!" she gasped. "Besides making yourself a killer, it wouldn't help Dad. Poole told Dad tonight that he had placed the facts in a lawyer's hands, that the minute anything happens to him, Dad will have to face that charge of murder." She waited, disheartened by the frown that gathered on Nick Treacher's high forehead. "You can't go up to the Ophir, either."

Nick said: "The clerk at the hotel knows me and won't give me away. I'll stay there. But I think there's something else I can do."

"Let me help," Mary said impulsively. "This is as much my fight now as it is yours."

Nick reached into his inside coat pocket and took out an envelope and a pencil. He tore off the back of the envelope, walked over until he was nearly within the rectangle of light coming out of the sheriff's office window, and spent a few brief minutes writing. Coming back to the girl, he picked up a rock and wrapped the paper around it along with a crisp dollar bill. He handed it to her.

"You can help," he told her. "Go to the railroad station and throw this, along with the money, through the window and into the ticket office. Try not to let the telegraph operator see who you are."

Mary looked down at the paper-sheathed rock in her hand. It seemed as though she was about to ask a question, but evidently she thought better of it for she merely nodded.

Nick said: "You can trust me. Tell your father that he's not to leave his house tomorrow morning, that there's an important reason why he should stay there."

His pulse quickened as her eyes raised to meet his. Mary Morgan's expression was one of intense relief, of warmth, almost of gladness. Some woman's instinct must have prompted her then, for she said, her voice barely above a whisper: "I'll never forget this, Nick Treacher." Then, before he could read her intent, she stepped close to him and kissed him full on the lips.

She turned and disappeared into the shadows before he had recovered from his surprise.

● ● ●

Three citizens of Strike were hard put to believe the things that happened to them in the twenty minutes that followed. The first, the telegraph operator, dozing in his chair before his instrument table, was jerked into abrupt wakefulness when an object sailed through his grilled window and struck him on the shoulder. His chair came to the floor with a bang. He looked stupidly around and finally saw the rock with the white scrap of paper and the dollar bill wrapped around it, lying on the floor near his chair. He picked it up, and his jaw fell open when he read what was written on the paper. It took him ten minutes to decide to send the message, and, when he did, it was with the muttered comment: "Well, I got paid for it, didn't I?"

The second, Jake Tolliver, night-clerk of the Boom-Town Hotel, couldn't at first make out the face of the man who came along the back hallway of the lobby and motioned to him from the foot of the wide stairway. When he did recognize Nick Treacher, he gasped in astonishment and came from behind his counter, hurrying his steps more than usual in walking over to the manager of the Ophir Mine. When Nick explained what he wanted, Jake grinned and growled: "I don't need this five dollars, Nick. I'd help you make a fool of Sam Poole for five cents. Sure you can have a room. Go up the back way and I'll meet you in the hall."

The third, Ed Wright, elbowing the bar alongside Sam Poole, was thinking that Poole's special brand of whisky was the best he'd ever tasted. But, an instant later, when Poole spoke, the whisky made Ed choke.

What Sam Poole said was: "Abe Stoops drifted in half an hour ago."

His words prompted Ed to push out from the bar, hands falling toward his guns. Ed was too late.

From behind him the barkeep spoke sharply: "Easy, stranger! This thing might go off!"

Ed turned slowly, careful now about his hands. He found himself staring into the twin bores of a shotgun.

Poole laughed softly. "It was a nice play while it lasted, friend. By this time Nick Treacher's broken jail. That's why I sent Luke over. And you're here. Maybe you'd like to take a little *pasear* up toward the Ophir with us."

Ed saw then how neatly this had been planned. It was late, and the Pay Dirt was deserted except for men he knew were in Sam Poole's pay.

"What's doin' up at the Ophir?" he drawled, as Poole reached out and flipped the guns from his holsters.

"A little matter between you and Curly Bates," Poole told him.

IV

Once during the night Nick Treacher was wakened by the sound of guns booming their thunder to the south of town, from up near the rim. He climbed from bed, went to his window that faced south, and looked off toward the Ophir.

Faint starlight was barely strong enough to show him the dark smear against the far slope that was the Ophir's shaft house. Below, at irregular intervals, he could make out the winks of powder flame that preceded the explosions. In the next five minutes he stood there watching, a little worried, only to find relief in the end when the firing slacked off and finally died out altogether. In the fifteen minutes longer he stood there, no gun spoke from up toward the rim. He went to bed again, confident that O'Reilly and the rest had kept the fences clear.

Two hours after dawn, a knock on his door roused him. Gun in hand, he threw the door open, stepped quickly out of sight.

Jake Tolliver came into the room, glanced, surprised, at the weapon in Nick's hand, then laughed nervously: "It's only me, Nick. I've got some news."

Nick tossed his weapon across onto the bed. Jake went on: "Curly Bates was cut down in that fight up by the Ophir last night. I thought you ought to know."

This was to be expected. Nick said: "Thanks for tellin' me about it, Jake. That's why I'm here, so Sam Poole couldn't say I did it."

"That ain't all," Jake said. "They've got a friend o' yours over in the jail. It seems Abe Stoops got loose and put Poole wise to who this gent was. I seen him when they brought him in. Gent about my size, looks like a cowhand. They had him roped to a horse and. . . ."

All at once Nick cut in: "Two guns, blue eyes, a flat-brimmed Stetson?"

"That's him."

Nick's pulse slowed before an emotion new to him, one of stark fear. He thought more of Ed Wright than of any man he knew, and now Ed was in danger, real danger, through loyalty to him. He didn't know how Abe Stoops had escaped from the Ophir's tool house. That didn't matter now. What did matter was that Poole would probably prove Curly Bates's murder against Ed.

Nick climbed into his trousers, pulled on his shirt.

"Anything I can do to help?" Jake asked.

"Keep your eyes and ears open, Jake. I'll be back later." Nick was swinging his shell belt about his lean waist, buckling it on. "Anyone out in the alley this time of day?" he queried.

"No one but the swamper peelin' spuds. He don't know you from Ulysses S. Grant."

"You might drop in at the Pay Dirt later on in the mornin', Jake. Whatever play Poole's makin' will start from there." Nick went quickly out the door, down the back stairway, and into the alley. He nodded pleasantly to the swamper who sat on the back kitchen steps with a knife in one hand, a potato in the other. He headed down the alley for thirty yards before he left it, cutting across a pasture that would lead him south, toward the rim.

Twenty minutes later Tim O'Reilly was swinging open the board gate in the high fence before the Ophir shaft house. O'Reilly's Irish face was set in a relieved smile. "Sure and it's good to see you back, Nick. Me and the boys was worried when we found out the sheriff had pried his way out of the tool house. And we didn't much like that powder burnin' last night."

"Anyone hurt?"

"Jensen. A slug nicked his shin. But he's on his feet."

Nick frowned thoughtfully, asking abruptly: "Tim, is all the shoring timber out of that old shaft?"

Tim, surprised at this irrelevant question, shook his head. "We've been too busy gettin' out the ore, Nick. I thought we'd let that go till we needed it."

Ten weeks ago, when Nick and his crew had started working the Ophir, he had abandoned work on the old shaft, that sloped downward obliquely into the face of the ridge. Instead, he had worked to deepen a new vertical shaft that the owners of the Ophir had been working when the decision was reached to cease operations. This new shaft, Nick already knew, was the only one that would ever be used in operating the mine, since the ore pocket almost certainly lay directly below and not at a slope from the shaft house, as the original operators had thought. But now he was thinking of the old shaft and its timbered stopes, where so much futile work and money had been spent in bringing out a low-grade ore.

"Tim, is that timber down there still dry?"

"Dry as a bone."

"Would it burn?"

"Would it? That's one of the things that's been worryin' me, Nick. I'm almost for forgettin' the timber down there and touchin' off a case o' giant powder to cave it in. We'll never work it."

"Not after today," Nick told him, and he went on to tell the Irishman of what had happened, of Ed's capture. Then he outlined a plan to Tim, one that brought a slow grin to the man's face and held it there until it had widened to a cunning smile.

But then Tim's smile faded suddenly before a look of concern. "You can't be doin' all that alone, Nick," he protested, only to be silenced as Nick went on.

Finally Tim O'Reilly nodded grimly. "If you want it that way, we'll do our best," was his answer to a question Nick had just put him. "Only you'd better pack some food in your guts before you start out."

Nick did take time to go to the cook shanty and eat a breakfast of wheat cakes and ham and coffee before he once more went out the gate and started down the hill trail toward town. He stopped once to call back to Tim O'Reilly: "You can touch the match in half an hour!"

Later, from the window of his room at the hotel, Nick Treacher saw the first faint haze of smoke that lifted from the cupola of the Ophir's shaft house. In five more minutes that haze had become a thickening smudge, climbing steadily to a black column over the Ophir.

A moment later he heard the first shouts out on the street. He smiled, satisfied that Tim O'Reilly's work with a barrel of coal oil poured on the timbers of the old shaft had been done well. That fire could burn as long or as briefly as Tim wished, for a few sticks of giant powder in the mouth of the old shaft would nicely close the opening until the fire burnt itself out underground. But until Tim got a certain signal, he and the rest of the Ophir crew would put on a good show of fighting that fire.

Nick waited at the window for ten more minutes, encouraged at the shouts and cries and the sound of boots pounding the walks out front. During that ten minutes he saw a thin line of men running up the hill trail thicken to an unruly, hurrying mob. The whole town now knew that the Ophir was on fire, and with the Ophir as one of the two mines in operation, the town was taking this fire as a major disaster. Not a man who climbed the hill relished the idea of having to pack up his goods and freight his family out of the country through lack of business.

When the street was comparatively quiet, Nick left his room and went down the front stairs and into the lobby. Jake Tolliver was sitting behind his desk at the counter.

"You know about the fire?" he asked Nick.

"I set it, Jake. What's the news from the jail?"

Jake's look was one of disbelief, but all at once he grinned, amused at some inner thought. "I couldn't get much," he said. "They spotted the fire while I was in the Pay Dirt gettin' my morning beer. Every damned man left the bar and went along with that crowd headed for the mine."

"Poole's men?"

"Luke Selden and three of his sidekicks went along. I saw Poole a minute or two later, headed across to the jail. He was in a hurry. Maybe that fire's got him worried, too, Nick."

"Did you hear what's going to happen to the man Poole brought in this mornin'?"

Jake nodded. "There was an awful mess o' free liquor bein' handed out in the Pay Dirt this mornin', along with lynch talk."

"That's all I wanted to know," Nick said, as he left the desk and headed for the front doors. Jake didn't miss the ominous sign of Nick's hand falling to the butt of his Colt, lifting the weapon partly out of its leather sheath, and then easing back again. It was the gesture of a man wanting to be certain that nothing would interfere with a quick draw.

At eight-thirty any other morning the benches in the shade of the cottonwoods in the courthouse square would have been partly filled with the oldsters, the men out of work, the loafers who had nothing better to do than seek the coolest resting spot in town to wait out the heat of the day. But today not one man idled on those benches. The square was as deserted as the walks in front of the stores.

The only sign of activity in the street was a two-team wagon that all at once skidded from an alleyway, the four horses at a run under the driver's swinging whip. In the bed of the wagon were six barrels, leaking water through their heads, bouncing heavily against the planks over the uneven street. The wagon turned right at the far end of the square, heading for the rim trail. Someone had evidently had the insane idea that the water in those barrels would help in fighting the fire at the Ophir. Glancing back once over his shoulder, Nick smiled in satisfaction at the mushrooming cloud of black smoke climbing into the blue void of the sky to the south. Tim O'Reilly was doing a great job.

Nick crossed the square, keeping out of line with the window of the sheriff's office. He reached the door to the office without once exposing himself. He twisted the knob, thrust open the door, and stepped in, right hand within two inches of the butt of his heavy .45.

The office was empty. His searching glance at once saw the bunch of keys on the sheriff's desk, the same keys he had used last night in locking Luke Selden into his cell. In five seconds he had opened the jail door and was stepping through it, smiling as he caught the startled, then relieved, expression on Ed Wright's face.

Ed stood behind the bars of the end cell. He breathed an oath and said: "Damned if you don't cut it thin, Nick." He stepped out through the cell door as it swung open.

"Too thin!" came a booming voice from the doorway behind.

Nick swung around, hand slashing toward holster. Ed, already facing the door, raised his glance. Then they both froze under the threat of Sam Poole's double-barreled shotgun.

Poole stepped into the jail, a smile on his face that was sneering, mirthless. Behind him, Abe Stoops stepped into the doorway opening, six-gun in hand. "You overplayed it this time, Treacher! That fire worked on everyone but me. You forgot how much I knew about the Ophir, about the old shaft. It's what's burnin', isn't it?"

Nick nodded but made no further reply.

"So it all gets back to where we started," Poole went on. "Only now there's two of you to stand trial for Curly Bates's murder."

"Think again, Poole. I slept in the hotel last night," Nick drawled.

Poole seemed unsurprised. "That won't make a difference. As operator of the Ophir, you're responsible for your crew. This partner of yours will have his neck stretched for the killing. You'll get at least five years as accessory to the murder. By that time I'll have mined out every cubic yard of pay dirt within the Ophir's boundaries. You won't wind up with ten dollars in your pockets."

"You ought to be able to think up a better one than that," Ed put in.

"Maybe I can." Poole frowned, obviously deliberating. All at once his black eyes flashed at some inner thought. He laughed harshly. He half turned, nodding to the sheriff. "You and I got wise to this play, Abe. We didn't hightail for the Ophir with the rest of the crowd. We were on the look-out for a jailbreak. We hid in that side entrance to the courthouse and saw

Nick Treacher come in here. When you came in after him, he already had this partner of his out of the cell. The partner had a gun. They saw you, opened up, and in the name of the law you cut 'em down. How does it sound?"

"Like I was pretty handy with an iron," Abe answered.

"How does it listen to you, Treacher?"

"Like you'll wind up at the end of a rope."

Poole laughed, shaking his head. "Not with my friend Morgan to swing the jury."

"I've got your story on Morgan," Nick told him. "He'll stand it so long and then buck."

"When he does, he's asking for the same as you're getting in about two minutes now."

The intensity of Poole's words, the mad killing lust that showed in his eyes, were signs that made Nick Treacher weigh his chances at drawing his single weapon and shooting it out. Only one thing made him hesitate: Ed stood here with him, unarmed, chained to these circumstances by loyalty.

"I'll make a deal with you, Poole," Nick said, seeing that the two round holes of the shotgun barrels had swung up and into line with his face. "Ed, here, isn't in this. Let him go and you've got my word for it he'll ride out of the country and never give away your play."

"You go to hell, Nick," Ed Wright drawled. "I'm in this belly-deep because I wanted to be." He looked across toward the door. "Don't let Nick run a sandy on you, Poole. I'm his partner . . . have been since yesterday. I get half of everything he takes out of the Ophir."

Nick said: "You're bein' a damned fool, Ed!" He knew he had failed, that Ed would be here at the end.

Poole all at once said gruffly: "Abe, you take the understrapper, I'll take Treacher." His thumbs drew back the hammers of the shotgun.

Nick felt the hackles rise along the back of his neck. He stiffened, right hand cocked to the draw, then he thought of something. "Better have Abe take a look outside," he drawled. "You wouldn't want witnesses to this, Poole."

"Thanks, friend," Poole said, meaning it. "Abe, see if we're alone."

The sheriff turned and walked toward the window of his office. This was the moment Nick Treacher had been playing for. His flat frame tensed, every muscle taut. He knew for a certainty that Poole would pull the shotgun's triggers, that he'd feel the slam of buckshot in his guts in the next split second. Yet he had a mad hope that he'd be able to lift his Colt free of leather, that he could toss it across to Ed and give him his chance.

As all this laid its clear pattern across his mind, as his brain willed his arm to move, he was suddenly pulled up by a low cry from Abe Stoops, out in the office.

"Boss!" Stoops called. "Morgan's on his way across here!"

Sam Poole said smugly: "Invite him in. He can be a witness to this."

"Damned if he sees me cut down a man," Stoops protested.

"Git back in here, Abe," Poole said dryly, "or I'll see you lyin' here with these other two."

A moment later Byron Morgan's voice was sounding gruffly from the doorway to the office: "Sheriff, where can I find Sam Poole?"

"In the jail," Stoops told him.

Morgan stepped into view, stopping in his tracks at what he saw.

"Come in, Judge," Poole said silkily, "you're just in time to witness the fact that Treacher and his friend were shot down while attempting a jail break."

"I'll witness plain murder," Morgan said testily.

"Aren't you forgetting something?" Poole reminded him.

Strangely enough, Morgan's grizzled face took on a quiet smile. "Sam, you're through," he said, reaching into a pocket of his coat and pulling out a yellow telegraph form, holding it out to Poole. "Read it!"

Poole, who had turned sideways so that he could keep his eye on both Morgan and Nick Treacher, said: "Read it yourself, Judge. I've got my hands full."

Morgan opened the telegram, glancing down at it: "This comes from Clovis, Poole. It says . . . 'You're not wanted for murdering me or any other man I know, Morgan. A sawbones took that bullet out of my lung twenty-four years ago, and I got well. I also found that you didn't rob me on that cattle deal. This gent Poole might be the man we know as Virginia City Poole, wanted for the sale of fraudulent mining stocks. Let me know.' Poole, this is signed by Fred Royer, U.S. Marshal."

Nick Treacher watched Poole carefully, noting the quick change that came over the man. Poole's blunt visage had lost a shade of color.

For a good five seconds, an ominous silence drew out. Morgan ended it by saying: "Put down that gun, Sam, or I'll blow your brains out."

Morgan, his hatred for Poole getting the better of him, had lost his sense of reason. He did a foolish thing at that moment, brushing his coat aside with his right hand, reaching for the butt of a six-gun that protruded from his hip pocket.

Sam Poole whirled in the doorway, his shotgun coming up to his shoulder. In that brief expanse of time, Nick Treacher yelled—"Drop, Morgan!"—and his hand blurred toward his holster, his palm hitting the ivory butt plates of the Colt and streaking the weapon up in a smooth, deadly swift draw.

Byron Morgan saw what was coming. Sobered by the threat of the swinging shotgun, hearing Nick Treacher's shouted words, he suddenly gave up all thought of the six-gun he'd dropped into his pocket less than half an hour ago. He fell clumsily, sideways, to the floor.

Two guns split the sudden silence with an inferno of sound. Nick Treacher's blasted out a fraction of a second before Poole's, the slam of his bullet in the man's side breaking the downward arc of the shotgun barrels as they followed Morgan's fall. It was the blow of Nick's bullet that caused Poole's muscles to tighten and pull the shotgun's triggers. The double charge of buckshot whipped over Morgan's head, taking out the lower half of the window up front.

The shotgun whirled out of Poole's hands. He stumbled, clawed wildly in under the lapel of his coat with his hand, reaching for the short-barreled six-gun in his shoulder holster.

As Nick Treacher swung his .45 in line with Poole once more, his thumb drawing back the hammer in an attempt to beat Poole's swift draw, Ed Wright suddenly threw himself forward in a rolling dive. At the exact instant Poole's weapon came down, Ed hit him at the knees, the weight of his hard-muscled body throwing Poole over backward.

Nick's shot prolonged the thunder of Poole's. Nick felt the air whip of a bullet above his head as Poole went over backward. Ed Wright's weight was partly responsible for Poole's falling. So was the heavy blow of Nick's bullet, for it took the man full in the chest, centering his white shirt front with a splotch of red that was already widening as he hit the floor.

Judge Morgan owed his life to the sheriff's heavy oak desk. Unwittingly he'd fallen behind it and given Abe Stoops a blind target to shoot at.

On the heel of Nick's second shot, Stoops opened up with two guns, his bullets driving obliquely down into the desk top, the shots filling the room with a beating concussion.

Ed, coming to his knees as Poole hit the floor, yelled: "Hold it, Nick!" A split second later he was wrenching Poole's six-gun from his hand, swinging it across and in line with the sheriff.

Stoops, stunned at seeing Poole sprawl backward out of the doorway, saw Ed's move too late. His hands were swiveling up his twin guns, lining them, as Ed's single shot slammed him back into the wall. Abe's hands opened, his guns fell, and he wrapped his arms around his middle as a groan came from his lips. As he fell forward, stiffly, blood gushed from his mouth.

Later, after Doc Spears had done all he could for the two dying men, Nick went into the courthouse and climbed the stairs into the steeple to run up the Territorial flag. That was the signal to Tim O'Reilly that he could blow in the entrance to the old shaft and choke out the fire. Nick waited up there five minutes. No explosion came, and the smoke thickened above the Ophir's shaft house. It was then that he saw the fringes of the crowd around the Ophir fence suddenly break and start down the hill trail, those in front running.

The next hour was the longest Nick Treacher ever lived through. The first word he had of the fire came from Nels Jensen, who was among the first back in town. Jensen, when he got his breath, said: "You'd better get up there, Nick. The old shaft caved, and some burning timbers dropped down into the new one. It's afire at the fourth level."

Nick left Ed at the sheriff's office with Morgan, hiring a buckboard and a team at the livery stable, making the drive to the Ophir in less than ten minutes. On the way up an ominous explosion shook the ground beneath the buckboard's wheels.

O'Reilly was the first man he met inside the fence. The Irishman's face was smeared with dirt and soot. He looked crestfallen, worn out.

"I had to do it, Nick," he said. "Dynamitin' the fire was the only hope we had of savin' her. The fourth level was blazin' to beat hell. I'm goin' down in the skip in a minute and have a look."

He walked away wearily, toward the shaft house. He knew as well as Nick Treacher that the dynamiting, necessary to save the mine, had wiped out any chance of getting any ore up from the sixth level they'd been working. Nick's chance to make good on his option had gone with the explosion as surely as though ten thousand tons of earth had caved in on the thin vein of silver-bearing ore they were working.

The smoke was gone now. Tom Baker's steam winch was working once more. Nick listened idly to the grinding of the winch's gears as O'Reilly took the skip down to the fourth level.

As he stood there, knowing that nothing he could do would help now, Nick felt a touch on his arm. He turned, irritable at the interruption. Mary Morgan stood alongside him, her finely chiseled face set soberly, a question in her eyes.

"I . . . I wanted to thank you for sending that wire to Clovis last night and saving Dad's life," she said softly. "Only I guess this isn't the time to do it. I heard what your man just told you."

Nick lifted his wide shoulders in a shrug, smiling down at her in a feeble attempt at unconcern. "I'm a gambler, Mary. I'll try my luck some place else."

By her look, the expression in her eyes, he saw that his words had somehow hurt her. He thought he understood what lay in her mind, yet now he wouldn't allow himself the hope that had come alive within him last night.

The grinding of the winch gears and the chugging exhaust of Tom Baker's donkey engine took his attention. The skip was on the way up, sooner than he'd expected. It could mean only one thing. Tim O'Reilly was on his way back with bad news.

Mary stood silently beside him, wordless in the same feeling of helplessness that had its hold on him. They stood together, probably for the last time, Nick was thinking, waiting for the inevitable word of defeat.

The clatter of the winch broke off. Suddenly the shaft house door flew open and Tim O'Reilly ran out, shouting something incoherent, waving his arms.

He came up to Nick, breathless, gasping: "The mother lode, Nick! As sure as I'm Missus O'Reilly's little boy Tim, it's the mother lode!"

Nick reached out, took Tim by the shoulders, shook him: "Tell it, Tim! Tell it fast! You're dreamin'!"

"Like hell I am! The cave-in on number four filled the shaft below, ripped out the shoring along the shaft. Nick, a million tons of rock cut loose. Half that rock is damned near pure silver. All this time we've been diggin' under the richest ore pocket in the Territory of Arizona. You're rich, Nick. Rich enough to buy out this town, the whole county." Tim took off his billed cap with its lit miner's lamp fastened to the front, and threw it high into the air.

Nick, unable to believe what he had heard, abruptly remembered Mary Morgan. Then he remembered something else. He turned to her, took her by the arms, looked down into her face, and caught her glad smile.

"You began something out there in the courthouse square last night," he told her. "Was it something you want me to finish, or . . . ?"

She shook her head, her face relaxing in mock-soberness. "No, Nick, not you." The gleam of excitement in her eyes belied her words. "After all, I started it. Isn't it up to me to finish it?"

Then, while he was still groping for the meaning behind her words, she raised her arms, put them about his neck, and lifted her face to his. But this time he kissed her back.

Forgotten Destiny

Jonathan Glidden completed work on "Forgotten Destiny" in late August, 1939. His agent, Marguerite E. Harper, submitted the story to Popular Publications on September 14, 1939. It was sold on December 28, 1939 for $90.00. It appeared in print as "Turncoat Gunman" in *Big-Book Western* (6/40). This story quite clearly anticipates the unusual artistry of future novels like *Gunsmoke Graze* (Dodd, Mead, 1942) or *Royal Gorge* (Dodd, Mead, 1948). The title has been restored, and the text is taken from the author's typescript.

I

Four days and three nights in the saddle had thinned Bill Duncan down a little. His heavy shoulders had lost a measure of their rope-muscled look, and his blunt face, usually bronzed and full and showing a perpetually good-humored expression, was now sun-blackened and sharp-planed and intently grave. The gray gelding he staked out in a spare patch of grass at Halfway Springs an hour after dusk that night was the fifth animal he'd ridden since leaving his lay-out near Arizona's southern border.

Near the water hole, he found dry brush for a fire and decided on a hot meal before he went on. In another hour or two the gentle breeze fanning the desert's hot sands would be chilled, and he could ride the last twenty miles into Rawhide in comparative comfort. He wolfed his meal and relaxed only when the second batch of coffee was simmering on the fire, promising further relief from the drowsiness crowding in on him. It was then that he remembered the money belt and crossed to the other side of the fire to take it from the pouch of his saddle and strap it about his waist beneath his shirt.

The clink of the gold coins in the belt reminded him once again of something that had puzzled him these four days. Tom Bostwick's letter had been casually worded. Bostwick was his father's old partner, and he had written a polite inquiry to ask whether Bill felt he could possibly lend him five thousand dollars—*for three months' time, after which I can sell some critters and pay you back.* The ominous part of the letter had been the enclosed promissory note, signed by Tom Bostwick, in the amount of five thousand dollars, that and the last two lines: *It would help some if you could get the money to me on the Fourteenth, a week from next Friday, providing this finds you well-fixed, and you can spare it.*

Tomorrow was only Wednesday, and Bill would get the money there in plenty of time. That wasn't what was worrying Bill. It was the promissory note. The fact that Tom Bostwick had enclosed it without any security whatever was mute evidence of an urgency the letter hadn't really mentioned. Because of the note, Bill might have read something between the scrawled lines that perhaps wasn't intended to be there—the fact that Tom Bostwick must be in trouble, real trouble. So, on the hunch that Bostwick would need a friend as well as hard cash, Bill had decided personally to deliver the money. He had dropped the rancher a line, telling him he was on his way.

That feeling of impending trouble was strong in him now as he hunkered down near his fire once again. It was that feeling that had made him hurry all this way, arriving two days ahead of time. His chunky frame made a squat shape against the shadows, and the jutting handle of a .45 Colt low along his right thigh gave him a menacing look that wasn't relieved by the bleak expression in his pale blue eyes. He was worried, and worry hardened his face.

The man who lay belly-down in the sand, barely twenty yards out from the fire and across the water hole, caught the flinty set to the face he saw framed in the notch of his Winchester's rear sight. It made him pause for a moment, and he found that his aim wasn't as steady as usual. Shortly he drew in a deep breath, let it out in a long, slow sigh, and squeezed the rifle's trigger.

The explosion of the shot slapped back in a sharp echo from the high rock outcropping beyond the fire. Bill Duncan swayed slowly and fell sideways without moving a muscle. He lay there huddled and still. Presently the man pushed up to his knees and squatted a moment, while levering another shell into the rifle's chamber. Then, rising all the way, he strode around the narrow pond and on into the circle of firelight and across to where Bill lay. The splotch of blood above Bill's left temple glistened wetly against the blond hair in the reflected firelight. It gave the man the only answer he needed.

He worked and pulled out Bill's shirt and roughly jerked out the money belt, cinching it to his own waist under his shirt. Without even a last glance at his victim, he walked beyond the fire, slung the saddle to his shoulder, and then moved out to where the gray was staked. Two minutes later, he had saddled the gelding and was riding south from the water hole.

Half a mile farther on, in the bed of a sandy arroyo, he changed from the gray to his own horse, a black with white-stockinged forelegs. Going on again, he led the gray by a rope tied to the animal's bit. He covered something over twenty miles before sunup, a distance that took him on a far swing to the south and east of Halfway Springs. Finally, when the sun was edging up over the far, flat horizon, he stopped long enough to loosen the gray's saddle cinch and break short the reins at hoof length. Then, shifting the saddle so that it was under the gray's belly, he slapped the animal across the rump and watched it trot aimlessly away. Satisfied with what he had done, he rode on, this time in toward a high rampart of hills that made a hazy blue bulk far to the northeast.

Sheriff Ben Alcott had often heard it said that any man who crossed this narrow neck of the desert by day was either a fool or fearful of what lay along his back trail. But, traveling it now, the lawman was neither of these. He was merely in a hurry, saving some three miles of the distance the roundabout trail through the hills toward Rawhide would have taken him.

In addition to being in a hurry, Ben Alcott was boiling mad. Usually he made a point of hiding any anger that might be in him. But now, alone, he didn't take the trouble. His light brown eyes, ordinarily spaniel-like in their docility of expression, were now flinty and with glinted surfaces. His gaunt face reflected an anger that, after all, was justified. Less than an hour ago he had suffered the worst indignity of his eighteen years as a lawman.

He was without his gun, usually as common a badge of his office as the five-pointed star that sagged from his upper left vest pocket. Along the left side of his face, high, near the prominent cheek bone, was a splotch of color a little darker than the rest of his weathered face. That bruise had been caused by the connecting force of a pair of knuckles. Those two things—the missing gun and the bruise—explained his anger.

He wasn't paying much attention to his surroundings. Now and then he urged his roan mare on to a faster pace in toward the blue line of the rim atop which the town of Rawhide lay. But he ignored the endless waste of sand and low rock outcroppings, the glare of the afternoon sun that had brought on a real thirst in him, the elongated shadows of the tall saguaro cactus and the dwarfed ones of prickly pear clusters and spiny yucca. He was wondering how best to explain his failure to serve the warrant he had that morning carried away from town with him, since the warrant was still neatly folded in his saddle pouch.

Had he been a little more conscious of his surroundings, the sudden shying of his roan wouldn't have come so close to unseating him. Nevertheless, he reacted almost instantly to this sign of nervousness from the animal, swinging his glance sideward to see what had caused it.

What he saw on a level with his eyes was the lined bore of a .45 Colt. Behind the gun, spraddle-legged on a low shelf outcropping, stood a short and solid man whose pale blue eyes were red-rimmed and fixed in a vacant stare. The man's square face was set in a grimace of pain. Seeing the matting of dried blood in the corn-colored hair above the left temple and the smear of caked blood down that side of the stranger's face explained the look to Ben Alcott. The lawman noticed then that the gun wavered in an unsteady hand.

It prompted him to say gruffly: "Swing that damned thing off me!"

His words seemed to focus the stranger's eyes. The stranger drawled: "I figured you'd sooner or later come up with me. Now it's my turn." With visible effort, his thumb drew back the hammer of the Colt.

Ben Alcott caught a warning sign in the sudden bleakness of those blue eyes. He didn't wait for more but kicked one boot from stirrup and started to roll out of the saddle on the off side of his roan. Behind him, the gun exploded in a burst of sound that racketed across the still, hot air. Falling, the sheriff felt the air whip of a bullet fan his bruised cheek. Then he was down, awkwardly, on hands and knees, mouthing an impotent curse as his roan shied away to leave him unprotected.

He wheeled toward the outcropping to see the gun swinging into line with him again. But now the stranger staggered, and his hand shook uncontrollably. He made an effort to reach across with his other hand and steady his aim, but abruptly his knees gave way, and he fell sprawling, face down. The arm that held the gun sagged over the ledge's edge, slowly the fingers relaxed their grip, and finally the weapon fell into the sand.

Ben Alcott let his breath out in a low whistle of relief. He came down off his knees and blotted the perspiration from his high forehead with a bandanna. He stepped over to pick up the weapon, unconsciously tapping the sand from the barrel end on his open palm. Reaching out, he took a hold on the stranger's hair and raised his head until he could look into the face. It was a young face, not ugly now that it was relaxed from the tight expression of pain. The red quality of the bronze on the skin, the fact that the stranger was hatless, told the sheriff that sunstroke and not the head wound had saved him from having to dodge a second bullet.

He carried the stranger to the back of the outcropping, and laid him in the shadow of the rock. He got his canteen and sloshed water into the stranger's face, forcing a little down his throat. But neither that nor a hard slap in the face caused even a flicker of the stranger's eyelids. Ben looked around for a horse and found none. Then he had his answer in the boot prints in the sand that led to the outcropping. This stranger had come here afoot, hatless, wounded.

The sheriff wasted no more time in conjecture. He lifted the stranger again, staggered across under his limp weight, and laid the man belly-down across the roan's withers. He steadied him with one hand as he swung up into the saddle. He rode out from the out-cropping in a direct line, and headed for Rawhide.

It was after seven that evening when the sheriff made the top of the rim trail and rode the half mile that put him into the beginning of Rawhide's wide street. Dusk softened the unrelieved ugliness of the nearly treeless street, and its shadows hid the untidy litter of the yards around the squat adobe houses at the edge of town. Farther in, the yards were neater. There were a few frame and brick houses with flower gardens behind picket fences. The heart of the street flanked the wooden awnings that showed at almost the exact center of town, where store lights were now winking against the gathering darkness, and the faint beat of a piano sounded from out of a saloon's swing doors. The walks down there were astir with life that cen-tered mainly about the hotel, the town's only two-story structure, and the two saloons, one on either side of the street.

Half a hundred yards short of the business section, Ben Alcott turned in at the tie rail before the adobe and rock jail. Two loungers on the walk near the door to the sheriff's office saw the body slumped over the roan's withers and drifted out to see what was the matter.

Alcott anticipated their curiosity by saying gruffly: "Lend me a hand here."

When they had carried the stranger inside and laid him on the cot in the first cell of the jail, the lawman didn't give the pair time to ask questions, telling them curtly: "Harvey, go get Doc Robbins. Fred, see if my brother's at home. If he is, tell him to get down here right away."

Because the lawman's manner was usually so mild, and now was gruff and commanding, the pair hurried out with the urgency of men who sensed that something out of the way was happening.

Doc Robbins was the first to arrive. By that time, the sheriff had hung a lantern above the stranger's cot and was sitting alongside it in a chair he'd brought in from the office. Getting up out of the chair, he nodded down to the unconscious man and told Robbins: "Found him wanderin' out there in the Bottleneck, Doc. No hat, no horse. He was out of his head . . . tried to shoot me before he keeled over. See what you can do for him."

Robbins saw the ugly wound at the side of the stranger's head, and reached down to push the hair aside and inspect it, muttering: "A bullet did that. How come"

"That's what you're here for . . . to find out."

The doctor sat down and opened the bag while Alcott brought a pail of water and some clean towels from the office. Then, hearing the street door slam as the doctor set to work, Alcott left the cell and went into the office, closing the jail door behind him.

The man who had come in resembled the sheriff in the way his eyes, the same shade as Alcott's, were set wide-spaced in his face. But there the resemblance ended, for his frame was portly, outfitted in a black broadcloth suit and white shirt in contrast to the lawman's dust-powdered blue denims and cotton shirt, and his manner wasn't docile like the sheriff's. Instead, he had a commanding air of authority. His face was flabby while Ben's bore a toughened look. They were brothers, but the eyes alone betrayed that.

Ben said gloomily: "No luck, John."

John Alcott's face reddened in sultry anger.

"Why not?"

"I went out there and had the handcuffs on Bostwick and was headed out with him. But I forgot about that young hellion of a girl."

"Ann? What about her?"

"We were comin' out of Bostwick's office when she stepped in behind me and shoved a Greener in my back. She called up the crew and gave them the guts they needed. They took my iron away and rawhided me off the place."

142

John Alcott's face was purple now. He took a cigar from a leather case savagely, bit off the end, and jabbed it in his mouth, clenching it between his teeth. "You're a hell of a sheriff, Ben!" he blazed. "Here I fix it up so we can swear out a murder warrant on Tom Bostwick, and you let him kick you around like he would a saloon bum."

"Not so loud, John," Ben said softly, nodding toward the jail door. He took the swivel chair at his scarred desk and tilted back in it. "You'll get Bostwick's lay-out. Only not through jailing him on a murder warrant. That would never stick. Tom Bostwick would never shoot at a man's back, not even that mangy sheepherder's they brought in yesterday. That was a fool idea to begin with, trying to saddle him with that killing."

"You've got a better one?" John Alcott scoffed.

"I have," Ben said bluntly. "Day after tomorrow you'll foreclose on the Wagon Fork. They'll call you a hard-hearted banker, but you'll have the outfit in the end."

"I've thought of that," the banker said impatiently. "Bostwick thought of it, too. He's sent for the five thousand."

"But he'll never get it."

Some of the banker's belligerence faded before a guileful questioning look. "What have you done now?" he asked in a voice edged with worry.

"I said Tom Bostwick would never get his money. That's all you need to know, John. Write up your fore-

143

closure papers. Go ahead on selling out the Wagon Fork to that sheep outfit. You can close the deal before the end of the week. Only don't forget how the deed is to be made out. We go halves on this."

A subtle change had come over the sheriff. His eyes were flinty, not soft. His words weren't spoken in the mild, almost ingratiating tones of a moment ago. John Alcott should have noticed that but somehow failed to. A light of greed was in his eyes now. But all at once he had a thought that made him say warily: "Understand, I'll have no responsibility in this. If anything goes wrong, I had nothing to do with it."

Ben Alcott's frame came lazily up out of the swivel chair, lazily but with an ease surprising in a man past fifty. "John," he drawled smoothly, "I sometimes wonder how yellow your hide is down the middle of your back. Get out. Get out before I forget my manners."

John Alcott backed toward the door, his slack face a chalky white. "Now, Ben . . . I didn't mean. . . ."

"Get out!"

The banker turned and hurried out the door, and his quick steps faded down the plank walk outside. The sheriff's grizzled face resumed its grave and disarming smile. He laughed softly and had turned toward the door to the jail when a sound on the street stopped him. He heard a horse turning in at the tie rail out front. He walked to the window and looked out into the street in time to see a thick-bodied man slope from the saddle of a black horse with white-stockinged forelegs.

He waited there at the window as the man came across the walk and through the doorway. He said: "Any luck, Ray?"

The newcomer wore a deputy sheriff's badge. His outfit was alkali-powdered and a two-day growth of beard darkened his coarse-featured face. He drawled—"Plenty."—and slapped his waist with an open palm. The clink of coins came from the blow his hand made in striking.

"All of it?" Ben Alcott queried.

Ray nodded. "Five thousand. It was easy. The coyotes are feedin' on him by now."

"What about his jughead?"

"Turned him loose down by the Tanks. One o' them greasers'll pick him up and feel lucky enough not to wonder where he came from."

Ben said—"Good."—and held out his hand.

Ray Mankey unbuttoned his shirt and fumbled inside it for a moment, then drew out a heavy money belt and handed it across. The sheriff went to a small safe that sat alongside his desk, worked the combination, and soon swung the door open. He tossed the money belt inside and locked the door again, saying when he'd finished: "Better get some sleep, Ray. You look like you need it. I've got a little something to attend to here."

He had started back toward the rear of the room and Mankey had turned to go out onto the street again, when abruptly the jail door swung open. Mankey stopped in mid-stride and stared curiously as Doc Robbins came into the office.

Robbins said—" 'Evenin', Ray."—and then looked at the sheriff, frowning. "Ben, I hardly know what to make of it," he said. "He's come to, and with a night's sleep he'll be all right. That gash in his head will heal up. But he's suffered a concussion. Doesn't remember a thing, not even his name."

"Who?" Mankey put in.

"A gent I found stranded out in the Bottleneck," the sheriff told him. Then, to Robbins: "Let's go in and have a look at him." He led the way back into the jail.

Ray Mankey followed out of curiosity. He stood in the jail doorway, looking in through the bars to the first cell in which the sheriff and Robbins stood alongside the cot at the back wall. From where Mankey stood, he could see only the legs and hips of the man who lay in the cot.

He heard the sheriff ask: "Feel better, stranger?"

"Some," the stranger's hollow voice answered. "But I can't remember."

"Take it easy," Ben Alcott said. "It'll all come back. Remember taking that shot at me out there this afternoon?"

"No."

"How'd you get there? You didn't have a horse and your skull was cooked plenty."

"Can't remember, Sheriff."

Ben Alcott stepped away from the head of the cot, out of line, so that Ray Mankey could see the stranger's face for the first time. The deputy caught his breath sharply on seeing that face and the blond head of hair that showed above the bandage.

The sheriff was saying: "You might as well bed down here for the night, even if you ain't under arrest." He turned to the doctor, saying: "Can you give him something that'll help him sleep, Doc?"

At that point Mankey cut in urgently: "Ben."

The sheriff turned questioningly. Mankey jerked his head toward the office and stepped back out of the doorway. Ben Alcott, puzzled, came out of the cell and followed. As soon as he had stepped into the office, the deputy pushed the jail door shut and breathed: "For the love o' God, Ben, do you know who he is?"

"No."

"It's him! The one I met at the springs last night! It's this Bill Duncan!"

II

For three long seconds Ben Alcott stood transfixed in a paralysis of sudden understanding. Then a black look crossed his face, and he breathed: "Then how come he's here? How come I found him fifteen miles this side of the Springs?"

Mankey shook his head, letting out a low oath. "Damned if I know. I had the side of his head in my sights, didn't even bother to make sure when I saw all the blood. He must have come to and started walkin'." He caught the coldly menacing look on the sheriff's face and added hastily: "I'll make good on this. The doc ain't goin' to be surprised if he cashes in by mornin'."

Ben suddenly motioned Mankey to silence as the jail door swung open. Robbins crossed the office and laid two white tablets on the desk, saying: "Give him both of these in a glass of water. They'll put him to sleep." He tucked his black bag under his arm and started for the street door. Halfway there, he thought of something that made him hesitate and look toward the sheriff again and ask: "How did you come out with Tom Bostwick today, Ben?"

"Not so good. His crew ran me off the place," Ben honestly admitted.

Robbins called: "Glad to hear it."

"I was sort of glad it happened that way myself," Ben said easily. "I told that sheep foreman he was loco when he swore out the warrant. Tom Bostwick never lined an iron at any man's back."

"But you went out there to arrest him," Robbins insisted.

Ben threw out his hands in a helpless gesture. "I couldn't help it. Sidney, the one that owns the sheep outfit, is a big augur down in Phoenix. I'd get my neck in a sling if I refused to serve any warrant his under-strapper swore out."

The doctor's face had gathered in a frown as Ben spoke. "How's it all going to come out?" he asked worriedly. "Are sheep going to take over this country?"

"Not if I can help it," the sheriff said grimly.

"What about Bostwick? Last directors' meeting at the bank, your brother claimed Tom wouldn't be able to pay up his note. With all the bad luck Bostwick's had, it means foreclosure. If he loses it, the sheep outfit will be the highest bidder to buy the place if he loses it. John will have to let them have the Wagon Fork because it's good business for the bank. As president, he can't do anything else."

"But he won't," Ben said. "Bostwick's got a man on his way in with the money to pay off his note. Fella by the name of Duncan, the son of one of his old friends over near the west end of the territory."

Doc Robbins's look was one of immediate relief. "That's good news," he said. "Well, I'll be by in the morning to have a look at our patient in there." He turned toward the door once more.

"What about this concussion, Doc?" Ben spoke up. "Will he ever come out of it and remember things?"

Robbins pursed his lips and stood a moment in thought. At length he shook his head, saying solemnly: "It's doubtful. An operation might relieve the pressure of the bone on the brain enough to bring back his memory. But, unless that or some accidental blow pushed that bone back into place, he'll always be like this."

"You mean, he'll remember only what happens from now on?"

Robbins nodded. "More than likely."

"Couldn't I try and get a line on him and find out who he is and bring him back that way?"

"It's possible but not probable, not with the blow that bullet gave him. He wouldn't know his own mother."

Ben shrugged. "That's tough," he said and stood there with his face set soberly and touched with sympathy as the doctor went out the door. Then, slowly, the sheriff turned to face Ray Mankey. His face broke into a broad smile.

"Ray, we're so damned lucky we stink," he drawled.

Surprise showed on Ray Mankey's face. "Lucky? How come?"

"You heard what Robbins said." Ben's voice was mildly excited now.

"Sure. What's there about that to get so het up over?"

Ben wheeled in through the jail door, saying: "Come along and I'll show you."

Bill Duncan lay on the cot, staring with unseeing eyes at the cell's ceiling. He turned his head as Ben, and then Mankey, came into the cell. He looked up into Alcott's honest face and drawled: "Thanks for bringin' me in, Sheriff. I reckon I'd have stayed out there for good if. . . ."

"Forget it," Ben cut in, waving the thanks aside. He pulled the chair next to the cot and sat down in it. His expression changed to a grave one, and he said solemnly, with telling abruptness: "I think I know who you are."

Bill elbowed up on the cot, sudden eagerness and hope mirrored in his eyes. He grimaced in pain once as he moved too quickly and his hand came up to the bandage around his head. But then he was smiling eagerly and said: "That's about the best news I ever had, I reckon."

Ben seemed unwilling to meet his glance. He looked back over his shoulder at Mankey. "Shall I tell him, Ray?"

After a moment, Mankey answered uncertainly: "That's up to you, boss."

Bill reached across and took a tight hold on the lawman's arm. "Get on with it!" he said harshly. "What's my name? Who am I?"

Ben let out a weary sigh. "I hate like hell to have to do this," he said. Then, with a shrug of his stooped shoulders, he stated flatly: "Your handle's Pete Brand. You're from Clayton, New Mexico. There's a price of fifteen hundred dollars on your head."

Bill's hand fell away from the lawman's arm. Some of the color drained from his face. He swung his feet slowly to the floor and leaned over with elbows on knees to bury his face in his hands. He sat that way for a long moment in which the silence dragged out awkwardly for all three of them.

Presently he raised his head. "What else?" he queried, and his voice had a hard and rasping edge to it.

"That's all."

"But how did you know all this?"

"I don't often forget a Reward dodger. Your picture was on one. It must've been three, four years ago. You're wanted for killin' an express messenger on the Santa Fé railroad."

"You're sure it's me, that I'm Pete Brand?" Bill voiced the name reluctantly, as though he loathed it.

Ben nodded. "You're supposed to travel with the Butch Olney gang. That fits, because Butch's wild bunch has been seen west of here lately, in the Mogollons. I figure you must have drifted over from there on a job of your own, maybe with a partner. Maybe you finished the job and were headed back. At any rate, you were shot and set afoot out there on the desert. That's the sort of a trick one of Butch's rats would frame on a man. 'Course, I'm only guessin'."

Bill seemed to be staring through the lawman now, frowning, in an obvious effort to get a hold on his memory. But in the end he shook his head and drawled in a flat voice: "Things aren't tickin' up there yet." He tapped his forehead with a forefinger. "Can't remember a thing."

"The doc said you wouldn't. But it's my duty to tell you you're under arrest and that anything you say will be held against you."

Bill's square face shaped a sardonic smile. His hand automatically went to a shirt pocket and pulled out a sack of tobacco. As his fingers thumbed out a wheatstraw paper and sifted tobacco onto it, he drawled: "There's nothin' much I can say, is there?"

"Nothin'," Ben said. He got up out of the chair. "Unless. . . ."

Bill looked up at him. "Unless what?"

The sheriff frowned thoughtfully. "I'm not sure yet. Let me think a minute." He turned to Ray, asking: "You think he'd do for the job?"

Mankey had enough elementary cunning in his

make-up to realize that he was to be the foil for some plan of the sheriff's, as yet unknown to him. He played on that hunch as he shrugged his knotty shoulders and said guardedly: "He might."

"What job?" Bill asked. He went on insistently: "See here, if you say I killed a man, shot him down in cold blood, you'll have to prove it, won't you? I mean, at the trial. I'll take my chances on standing trial. I think you're wrong."

Ben said: "Wait a minute. I'll prove it right now. I don't think I threw that Reward notice away. Watch him, Ray." He went out of the cell and into his office. They heard the rattle of the desk drawers out there. Bill finished building his smoke and lit it, offering the makin's to Mankey, who shook his head.

Presently Ben Alcott came back in through the office door. He had a dog-eared sheet of paper in his hand, and held it out to Bill. Bill saw that it was a Reward dodger, and the stubbornness that had been in his face a moment ago faded before a look of doubt as he read the printed words. Finally he said: "The description might fit. But you can't tell a thing from the picture. It's blurred."

Ben shrugged. "Here's wishin' you luck. But it's my private opinion that you're this Pete Brand. We'll know for sure as soon as I've wired for Santa Fé to send in one of their detectives and identify you."

Bill crumpled the Reward notice as he clenched his fist. He looked at the sheriff, seeing nothing but reserved sympathy on the thin, grizzled face. For a moment his former stubbornness returned but finally gave way to the growing uncertainty. It was plain he was trying to remember, and couldn't. He said: "I don't feel like a man who'd take to his guns at the drop of the hat. That don't fit."

"Maybe the bang on the head cured your cussedness, Brand," Alcott suggested.

Bill seemed to remember something then. "A minute ago you mentioned a job. What kind of a job can you give a prisoner?"

"I was a little hasty," the sheriff said cautiously. "You didn't seem like a bad sort until I happened to remember that thing." He pointed down to the Reward notice. "I was thinkin' maybe I could use you."

Bill said nothing, unable to read the workings of the lawman's mind.

Presently the sheriff said in his mild tone: "I've never been a bounty hunter. The county pays me a hundred a month, and I save half that. So I wouldn't know how to use the reward money on you, if I had it, except to bank it and leave it to my kinfolks, who don't need it anyway." He fixed an examining look on Bill, one that was prolonged and open. Then, seeming to make a sudden decision, he went on: "I'm past fifty, and by now I ought to know men. It don't strike me that you're as mean as that Reward notice makes you out. You're young, too, young enough so that a stretch in Yuma would do you plenty of harm, if I sent you there. Supposin' I give you a chance? Will you do me a favor?"

Bill laughed mirthlessly. "Feed a stray dog and he's yours whether you want him or not."

Once again Ben looked back over his shoulder at Ray Mankey. His deputy gave a slow nod of his head and said: "It's up to you, Ben."

The sheriff faced Bill again, and this time his manner showed that he'd decided something. "All right, Brand, here it is. I want to see you make a new start, get clean out of this country and into another where you won't be known. It's my opinion that a law officer can do his job better by playin' along with a man than by always bein' ready to collect the reward on him. So I'll let you go. But first you've got to do something for me. There's a warrant I want served on a rancher north of here, man by the name of Tom Bostwick. It's a murder warrant, and the man that brings Bostwick in will have to be pretty level-headed. Bostwick's got a salty crew, and they'll tear you to pieces if they know who you are."

"That's why you haven't brought him in?" Bill asked.

Ben smiled guiltily. "Fact is, I was out there today. I had the handcuffs on Bostwick and was bringin' him out of the house when his daughter rammed me in the back with a shotgun. She held me there while she called the crew. They took my iron away and rawhided me off the place."

Bill was frowning. At length, he said: "So this Bost-wick's a murderer?"

"No, he ain't. But one of the crew is. Three days ago

a sheepherder was found lyin' along Wagon Fork's fence with a bullet in his back. Since Bostwick has had trouble with the sheep outfit ever since they moved in next to him this spring, it's a fair bet that one of his men did the bushwhackin'. The foreman of the sheep crew swore out a warrant on Bostwick on a technical charge of murder. We'll arrest him and hold him until he admits who did the job. Either that, or until I find out for myself."

There was real relief on Bill's face now. "That's not so bad, then. When do you want me to go out there. Tonight?"

Ben shook his head. "Get some sleep and go out in the mornin'. But here's something else. I've thought of a way for you to get into Bostwick's place and take him out right in front of his crew. Ever hear of Bill Duncan?"

He put the question abruptly, and, as he watched Bill, his glance hardened. He was looking for the mention of Bill's name to bring back some glimmer of memory. But it obviously didn't. Bill's look didn't change, and finally he shook his head, saying: "Never heard of him."

"Thought you might have," the lawman said, nicely concealing his feeling of genuine relief at having hurdled this last remaining stumbling block. "He's from over west of here, near where that wild bunch of yours has been hangin' out. Young Duncan is on his way here right now with five thousand dollars Bostwick needs to pay off a note he's carryin' at the bank. Bostwick's had some bad luck this summer with cattle and the bank's callin' his note. So he wrote an old friend, the father of this Bill Duncan, askin' for the money. The old man was dead, but the son offered to stake Bostwick and bring the money over himself. I want you to go in to Bostwick's, tell him you're Bill Duncan. It won't be hard to get him alone, arrest him, and bring him in without his crew savvyin' what's up until it's all over."

"But he'll know I'm not Bill Duncan."

"He won't know anything. He's never seen Duncan, not the younger one. You're about the age he ought to be, and you can put it across. You needn't worry about Duncan turnin' up to spoil your play, either. He isn't due for a couple of days yet."

"What'll I say about the money?"

Ben frowned, as though not having thought of that. Then he said: "Maybe this'd work. You'll have that bandage on your hand. Why not tell Bostwick you were followed across the desert and shot and robbed of the money? He'd swallow that."

Bill considered and said: "I can sure try."

Ben Alcott looked down severely at Bill a moment before his glance softened. "Hope I'm not makin' a mistake, lettin' you go, Brand," he said. "I'll stake you to a horse and a hull, once you've got Bostwick back here. Maybe after that you'd better head up into Utah. It's easy for a man to lose himself in that country."

Bill's expression was one of real gratitude. He said solemnly: "I'll never forget this, Sheriff. And I sort of hope I'll never remember what I was before today. It'd be hard, havin' a thing like that to live with."

"If that bump on the head's made an honest man out of you, I'm hopin' the same. One thing more. You needn't worry about anyone here rememberin' your name. People in this country never heard of Pete Brand." He took down the lantern, nodded to Ray, and said: "Let's let him turn in."

They went out, Ben locking the cell and jail doors. In the office, Ray Mankey went to the far wall to sit in a chair near the desk, a broad smile on his ugly face and shaking his head as he eyed the sheriff. "Damned if you don't take the cake, Ben," he said. "You should have been a parson. How in hell did you think up that gag on the Reward notice?"

Ben said: "It's a habit of mine to remember things like that."

Ray nodded admiringly. "It may work." All at once his look sobered. "What'll we do with him after he's brought Tom Bostwick in? If we let him go, he's likely to remember someday and come back and raise some trouble."

"That's where you come in, Ray. You'll have to do your job all over again."

III

Bill did some plain and sober thinking on his way out the Wagon Fork trail at noon the next day. He'd had a good night's sleep, the doctor had changed the bandage on the bullet-gash along his scalp, and his head didn't hurt so much now. His thoughts had seemed to be running a little clearer this morning.

Ben Alcott had treated him like a white man, trustingly. He'd given him a horse, this long-barreled, unbranded buckskin, bought him a new Stetson, and even returned his gun. This morning the sheriff hadn't once reminded him of his past. Aside from calling him by his right name, Pete Brand, there hadn't been any reference to last night's conversation in the jail cell. The only pains the lawman had taken was in schooling him for the part he was to play in meeting Tom Bostwick today, assuming the name and character of Bill Duncan.

Bill was grateful for the lawman's kindness. Now, taking a climbing trail through a light stand of tall timber that covered the slopes below Wagon Fork's high mesa pastures, Bill knew that he would make good on this chance Alcott was giving him. He was impatient to finish the job of bringing in Bostwick. The sheriff had said: "Tom's a nice old gent. Friend of mine, has been for years. Don't let him soften you up and get you to feeling sorry for him. Just remember, it isn't him that's really in trouble. It's the man that shot that sheepherder. We're usin' Bostwick as bait."

Once he'd returned the favor the sheriff was doing him, he'd head out of this country and ride as far from it as horseflesh would take him. He was hoping he'd never remember the past, never again become the man the real Pete Brand must be, the hardened killer, the outlaw.

Bill was curious about one thing, and finally that curiosity became so strong that he gave way to it. He let his hand fall smoothly to the leather sheath at his thigh and palmed up his Colt. He was a little surprised at the ease with which he made the first draw. He tried it again, letting his hand move faster. The gun rocked into line at his hip with the fleeting speed of thought. It made him a little afraid, and then and there he decided never to use this uncommon gun swiftness, never again to turn his gun on a man unless he was forced to. Once he was clear of the country, he could stop packing a gun at all and in that way remove any temptation for using one.

He topped the trail's upslope and had his first glimpse of Wagon Fork's nearest lush grass pasture. It roused in him an instinctive and forgotten feeling of admiration, and he knew then that, whatever else lay along his back trail, he did have a range-bred eye and a knowledge of good grass when he saw it. Here, where the trail came onto the mesa, the timber went on for half a hundred yards before the meadow opened out. Across there, two miles away, he could make out a sprawling cluster of buildings of weathered board and adobe and knew that he was looking at Wagon Fork's headquarters. It had the look of a prosperous outfit. He remembered Ben Alcott's saying that Tom Bostwick had had some bad luck in cattle this summer and decided that it must be the higher hill meadows that had been hit badly by the long summer drought.

He had reined in on the buckskin and was sitting

there, idly letting his glance inspect what lay ahead, when all at once a voice said from behind him: "Like the looks of it?"

Turning in the saddle to face that voice, Bill was surprised at its low musical quality. Even before he saw the girl, standing near a thick stand of lodgepole pine, he knew that he wasn't going to see a man.

The first thing that caught his eye was the Winchester cradled in the crook of her left arm. Next, he saw that her slender hand was closed over the rifle's breech, thumb on hammer and second finger crooked about the trigger. His glance lifted to her face. It was oval, clean-featured, and grave but set in an expression of wariness. Hazel eyes regarded him with a faintly hostile stare.

This girl was remarkably pretty. She wore a denim skirt and a red-and-white checked shirt open at the throat. She was tall and her figure gently rounded and boyish-looking. A sliver of sunlight penetrating the light shadows beneath the tree touched her chestnut hair and framed her face with fine-spun copper.

"Sure I like it," Bill drawled. "Who wouldn't?" As an afterthought, he added: "You must be Ann Bostwick."

She nodded.

He said: "Still on the warpath?"

Interest and an increased wariness flared alive in her eyes. "Who told you I was on the warpath?" she asked.

Once again he was struck by the rich tone of her voice. "Ben Alcott."

The mention of that name brought an instant's hostility to her glance. "Did the sheriff send you up here?" Her tone was no longer pleasant.

Bill shook his head, and his blunt face took on a disarming grin. "No, but I heard about it last night. Yesterday must've been Alcott's unlucky day. First he gets kicked off your place and last night he loses this horse to me at a game of draw."

Her look changed subtly. "Then who are you?" she asked.

"Bill Duncan."

The last trace of her hostility faded before an open, warm smile. Her hand moved away from the rifle's breech, and she even took one impulsive step toward him before she caught herself. Her face deepened a shade in color, and she breathed: "Bill Duncan. Then you're here at last." There was a gratefulness and relief in her voice he didn't miss. "Dad thought you might be too late. His note's due tomorrow." All at once a hurt surprise came into her eyes as she saw for the first time the bandage showing beneath the Stetson-brim. "Something's happened to you. You've been hurt."

Bill nodded, deciding to come at once to the point. "I reckon I've made a mess out of it, miss. Two nights ago a gent paid me a call at my camp out on the desert. He was obligin' enough to shoot me and save me the trouble of carryin' my money belt the rest of the way."

Ann Bostwick's face blanched, and her eyes were

wide in sudden alarm. "Then . . . then you haven't the money?" she asked incredulously.

He shook his head. "No."

She came toward him now, standing close to his stirrup and looking up at him, first with a pleading in her hazel eyes, and then that look changing to one of utter bewilderment. "What can we do?" she said finally in a barely audible voice.

He lifted his shoulders in a shrug. "It's got me stumped," he admitted. "But I thought I'd come on anyway. I wanted to explain to your father."

For a long moment they looked at each other. Her glance changed, and now there was nothing but sympathy in it. She said, forcing a smile: "Of course, you did all you could. I . . . I'm sorry I had to act this way." She held out her hand, and he took it, for the moment ashamed of the part he was playing as he felt the firm grip of her slender fingers. "You're to call me Ann. And you're Bill, aren't you? My pony's over there." She nodded back into the trees. "Wait here and I'll be back in a minute."

They made the two-mile ride across to the lay-out in near silence. Only once did the girl speak, and then only because she seemed to think that her presence back there along the trail needed explaining. "Dad's eating. I was watching the trail while he was gone."

"Expecting trouble?" Bill asked.

"We had it yesterday, didn't we? Ben Alcott might try it again. It's ridiculous, Dad charged with murder."

"The way I get it, it isn't really him they're after."

She shrugged wearily and said: "We don't know what they're after. Ben Alcott has always been friendly to Dad. You wouldn't think he'd turn against us now, especially with that sheep outfit waiting to take over the place."

"Sheep?"

She said—"Yes, haven't you heard?"—making Bill wonder if this wasn't Bostwick's way of working off the grudge hard luck and falling cattle prices had saddled on him. He made no comment, remembering why he was here, and not wanting to add any more weight to the momentary feeling of uncertainty the girl's mention of the sheep crew had given him, for her remark had brought up in him the instinctive hatred of the cattleman for the sheepman.

They rode along a poplar-bordered lane beyond the outbuildings and in toward the house. He came out of the saddle to open a gate alongside the lane's cattle guard, and it was while he was closing the gate that he looked toward the low and sprawling adobe house to see a man come out of the center doorway and walk out across the clean-raked yard toward them.

"There's Dad," Ann said in a low voice. "I wish he didn't have to know. But he might as well hear it now as later."

Tom Bostwick was a man of big stature, massive about the shoulders and with white hair and a grizzled, longhorn mustache that gave him a distinguished look. His walk was the rolling gait of the saddle-bred man. His bronzed and rugged face had a hawkish,

164

aquiline set of features. In his eyes, brownish-green like Ann's, was a quizzical, but kindly, look as they rode in toward him.

"Dad, this is Bill Duncan," Ann said as she reined in alongside her father.

Tom Bostwick's glance showed sudden and genuine gladness. He thrust out a big hand as Bill sloped from the saddle. His massive fist clenched Bill's solid one in a vise-like grip. "You look like your old man, Bill," he said cordially. "Glad to know you." Then, sensing something out of the way in his daughter's manner, he looked at her, and his glance became puzzled as he queried: "Why so grim?"

Ann tried to force a smile but couldn't. "Dad," she said weakly, "he . . . Bill lost the money."

Bostwick's glance whipped back to Bill. At first his eyes showed bitter disappointment. Then there was grim resignation in his glance. "What happened, Bill?"

Bill again gave the story Ben Alcott had told him that morning. Bostwick at first listened intently, then with his face taking on quick anger. As Bill finished, he breathed a low oath and asked: "Where were you camped, there at the Springs? How did he come up on you?"

Here was something the sheriff had neglected to give Bill, a description of Halfway Springs. Bill paused in making his answer, saw that Bostwick noted his hesitation, then said quickly: "To the south of the Springs. Whoever shot me was layin' out there in the dark. When I came to, I walked on back and saw where he'd bellied down."

A hint of puzzlement flared alive in Tom Bostwick's eyes now. "To the south of the Springs?" he said. "How far were you camped from the pond itself?"

"Close in. Maybe fifty feet."

The working of Tom Bostwick's mind was plain on his face. At first his expression was puzzled, then there was bewilderment written there, finally disbelief. "You're sure about that? It was fifty feet?" he drawled.

Bill sensed that he had made a mistake, a grave one, for the rancher's manner was no longer friendly. He said impatiently: "It was dark. Maybe I've got it wrong."

"You sure have," Bostwick said. "Because fifty feet from the pond would mean you made camp on the top of a sixty-foot rock outcrop." He waited and, when Bill made no reply, asked abruptly: "Who sent you here? Who are you?"

"I'm Bill Duncan."

Bostwick's face took on a tight smile that lacked all amusement. He made a motion of his hand to warn back a protest he saw coming from Ann who had dismounted and was now standing to one side. Then, without taking his eyes from Bill, he called back over his shoulder: "Slim! Get out here!"

A tall, angular man wearing a pair of holsters slung low along his flat thighs stepped out from around the nearest corner of the house, less than forty feet away. He came on four paces, then stopped, thumbs hooked in his belts. He was standing to one side of Bill and Tom Bostwick, on Bill's right, and his inscrutable gray eyes seemed to focus on Bill's waist as he drawled: "What'll it be, Tom?"

"Watch this man!" Bostwick's face had settled into a dogmatic look, and, as he spoke to Bill, his voice was deep-toned, curt. "If you're Bill Duncan, you'll know who Sam Singleton was."

Bill didn't know who Sam Singleton was. Eyeing Slim, he said flatly: "Get that man out o' here, Bostwick!"

Ann spoke from off to his left: "Answer Dad's question! Who was Sam Singleton?"

In that instant Bill knew he had lost, that the sheriff's ruse hadn't worked. A cool nervousness was in him as he tried to gain time, drawling: "You tell me."

Tom Bostwick said scornfully: "How much is Ben Alcott payin' you to come up here and try takin' me? Sam Singleton was the brother of Bill Duncan's mother." He eyed Bill coolly a brief moment, then called to his crewman: "Slim, I'm goin' to. . . ."

Bill's lunge caught him in mid-sentence. He made a futile effort to dodge back out of the way. Then Bill was in behind him, left arm closed hard about his waist, and he felt the prod of a gun's barrel in his back as Bill turned him roughly to face him. Slim's guns were out now; the tall man was ready. But the rancher's bulk shielded Bill from him.

Bill called: "Drop the hardware, Slim! I'm takin' Bostwick out with me!"

Behind Bill, Ann said in a casual voice: "I'll count three before I shoot you in the back! One . . . two. . . ."

"Go ahead!" Bill drawled. "This iron's got a hair-trigger!"

"Ann!" Tom Bostwick's voice exploded. "Put down that gun!"

"But, Dad . . . !"

"Put it down, I say!" The rancher's voice had a hard, commanding edge to it. "Slim, don't force his hand. He's a killer. I'll go with him."

Slim's look was one of stunned disbelief. He had opened his mouth to protest when Ann's voice cut in: "Do as he says, Slim! We're licked!"

Without slacking the pressure he put on the gun thrust against Tom Bostwick's spine, Bill pulled the rancher around so that he could see both Slim and the girl. He was facing the house. Two more men had appeared to witness this, one who stood in the center doorway of the ranch house, the other in the stretch of open yard beyond the wall corner around which Slim had stepped a few moments ago.

Bill drawled: "Tell your boys to behave, Bostwick!"

"Stay out of this, all of you!" the rancher called. At his word, Slim shrugged resignedly and dropped his guns, and the man behind Slim in the yard stopped the move his hand was making toward holster.

Bill saw the barrel of the girl's rifle lower slowly until it pointed to the ground. She said lifelessly: "What will you do with him?"

"Take him to the jail and keep him there until after

the sheriff finds out who killed that sheepherder," Bill told her.

"But we don't know!" Ann said hotly. "Our men didn't do it! They've framed this on Dad to get him out of the way while they foreclose on the place."

"I wouldn't worry," Bill told her, taking two backward steps toward the horses and pulling the rancher along with him. "There's still this Bill Duncan."

Tom Bostwick slowly shook his head. "We'll never see Bill Duncan," he stated with conviction. "He was due yesterday. Something's happened to him."

As he tried to make sense out of the rancher's words, remembering that Ben Alcott had last night claimed Bill Duncan wasn't due for two more days, Bill tried to put down the instinctive liking he had for these people. Tom Bostwick was all man, and he had recognized it at first sight of the rancher. He hadn't defined his feeling toward the girl, didn't want to, for she was attractive to him, and he wasn't willing to recognize that, faced as he was with a duty he owed the sheriff. So now he said curtly: "Get back, all of you! Back there by the door where I can keep an eye on you."

They hesitated, until Tom Bostwick put in: "It's no use. You'd better do as he says. Ann, forget that rifle. It won't do any good now."

Reluctantly the man in the yard behind Slim moved in toward the door. Slim said flatly—"Stranger, I'll be in town tonight lookin' for you."—and followed. Ann was the last to move. She gave her father an eloquent

169

look of pleading, but his slow shake of the head made her turn and walk in toward the doorway. Her head no longer had its proud tilt, and she didn't look back again.

Bill said: "Take her pony. I'll go first."

He backed away from Bostwick, in alongside the buckskin, and then around behind the animal. He watched Tom Bostwick step over to his daughter's paint horse and climb stiffly into the short-stirruped saddle. He jerked his head to indicate that the rancher should come in between him and the house, and, when Bostwick's pony had covered the distance, he vaulted into his own saddle and started the buckskin out across the yard in the lead. He had a few bad seconds opening the gate by the cattle guard but managed to keep Bostwick's paint pony between him and the watchers in the doorway.

Then they were clear, around a turning in the lane and the house out of sight. He drew rein and let Bostwick ride even with him. He rested the .45 on his saddle horn and looked across at the rancher.

Bostwick said in bitter sarcasm: "You've done something to be proud of, stranger! You've knocked the props out from under one of the best outfits in the territory."

"Better save your talk until it'll count for more," Bill advised, nicely hiding the fact that Bostwick's words had struck home to him. He wasn't proud of what he'd done.

IV

"There's a thing or two I don't understand about this," Bill told Sheriff Alcott in the jail office at dusk that evening. The lawman had just come out of the jail after locking Tom Bostwick in the cell Bill had occupied last night. Bostwick hadn't said much, but the few words he had spoken had only increased Bill's puzzlement over certain things he had heard today that didn't quite fit with the sheriff's story. He was going to get things straight now.

Ben Alcott was tilted back in the swivel chair at his desk, his face shadowed by the failing light that came through the office's single window on the street. He said: "There's plenty I don't understand myself. I hate this about as bad as anything I ever had to do. You heard what Bostwick said. Him and me have always been friends, not close but friends anyway. Now he says I've turned on him. He blames me for lockin' him up. Says I'm workin' with my brother and the bank to help foreclose on his outfit." He gave an eloquent shrug of his narrow shoulders. "Makes me feel like hell."

"You claimed last night that this Bill Duncan wasn't due for a couple of days. Bostwick says he was due in here yesterday."

"It's his guess against mine. He got that letter from Duncan two days ago and told my brother at the bank about it. I reckon he figured Duncan would wear out half a dozen jugheads gettin' here from clear across the territory. I figured he'd take his time, maybe pull in on the date the note is due, tomorrow. I was right, and he was wrong. I played that hunch when I sent you out there today."

Bill considered this and was satisfied, since the sheriff's argument was logical. "What's the set-up on this sheep outfit?" he queried, voicing another doubt that had been put in his mind today. "Both Bostwick and the girl claim the bank's ready to sell that graze over to sheep."

"That's the bank's business. Only with Duncan on his way in, they can't sell the Wagon Fork out from under Bostwick. Besides, what're you worryin' about? You've earned your parole, Brand. Don't sit there bellyachin' at me when all I've done is my sworn duty," he said in an injured tone. "There was a warrant out for Bostwick, and I served it, or you did, which amounts to the same thing. Bostwick's where he belongs, and you've earned your parole."

This abrupt reminder served to put down any last doubt that remained in Bill. He saw Ben Alcott as a sincere man honestly trying to do his duty even though he had to risk Bostwick's friendship in carrying it out. He felt a little sorry for the seemingly harassed lawman. "I wasn't meanin' to ride you," he said apologetically. "Only I wanted to get things straight."

"You'll never get 'em straight, so don't try," Alcott told him. "These local politics won't bear meddlin'

172

with." He got up out of the chair and went to the door to open it and look along the street, asking abruptly: "That head of yours feel all right now?"

"Good as ever."

"Did the ride out there today bother you any?"

"No. Why?"

"I was thinkin' that Tom Bostwick has some friends around here who saw you bring him in. It might not be so good for you to hang around. If you feel like it, you could start makin' tracks north tonight."

Bill said: "Then you're really turnin' me loose?"

"I said I would, didn't I? I generally keep my word." Alcott closed the door and came over to light the green-shaded lamp on his roll-top desk. He went to his knees beside the small safe nearby, adding: "You'll need some money. Fifty dollars ought to last you until you've landed work. I'd appreciate gettin' it back again if you ever have it to spare."

He had opened the safe's door and now took out a money belt. He opened a flap of one of the pouches and spilled out into his hand a dozen gold coins. Handing five of them across to Bill, he returned the rest to the pouch and then the belt to the safe again, closing the door and spinning the combination.

Bill's emotion at this show of generosity made it hard for him to find words. But finally he said: "I'll never forget this, Sheriff."

"Here's hopin' you won't," Alcott said. "It's worth this and plenty more to see a man started straight." He nodded toward the door. "Better be hightailin'."

Bill wanted to say something, to add more weight to the feeble thanks he'd already given the lawman. Alcott must have understood for he slapped Bill on the back and pushed him gently toward the door, saying: "Forget it!"

Bill went out into the street, turning once on his way across the walk to see the lawman standing by the office window. He raised a hand in salute after he had swung into the buckskin's saddle. Then he was wheeling the buckskin out into the street, and the jail was behind him.

He took the trail he had that morning followed toward Wagon Fork as he walked the buckskin out the end of the street. A hundred yards beyond the last adobe house of the town, he caught distinctly the sound of trotting ponies coming toward him along the trail. Instinctively he reined the buckskin to one side and rode ten yards beyond before he turned again in a line that paralleled the faint markings of the trail.

Shortly the shapes of three riders came out of the deep shadows up ahead. They had drawn almost abreast of him before he recognized the tall and thin shape of Slim, the Wagon Fork crewman Bostwick had summoned from behind the house this afternoon. Slim was leading a riderless pony.

Bill tightened his grip on the reins and brought his horse to a stand, leaning far forward in the saddle and clamping his hand on the animal's nose to stop him from whickering. He stayed that way until the hoof sounds of the four ponies had died out along the street and only then straightened, considering an idea that had come to him at his first sight of Slim and the riderless led horse.

Ben Alcott was alone there at the jail. Mankey was away somewhere. Slim and the other pair might have been riding into town merely out of curiosity to see what had happened to Tom Bostwick, but if that was their only reason, why the led horse?

Suddenly Bill realized that here might be his opportunity of canceling the debt of gratitude he owed Rawhide's sheriff. On the heel of that thought he reined the buckskin around and clamped his spurs to the animal's flanks. He didn't go back to the trail but struck in toward the narrow rectangles of light coming from the store lights shining along the narrow passageways between buildings at the town's center. In less than thirty seconds he came abruptly into the alley that backed the buildings on the jail side of the street.

He left the buckskin tied to the top pole of a corral fifty yards below the jail's squat outline and went on at a run, not slowing his stride until he had passed the jail's near corner. He went along the rear to the far corner, and then wheeled up the narrow passageway that separated the building from its neighbor. He stopped a stride short of the passageway's street end, flattened his frame against the wall, and edged out until he could look across to the hitch rail.

Four horses were standing there. Three of the saddles were empty. A man sat astride the fourth, holding the reins of the other three and looking nervously up and down the street. Bill saw that the street was practically deserted here, since the town's two saloons and the hotel were a hundred yards below, flanked by the few stores still open. The jail, out of the center of town, would be well out of sight of any after-supper idlers along the walks. Slim must have known that in bringing his men arrogantly to the jail hitch rail.

Bill's right hand was lifting to the handle of the Colt along his thigh when the screen door to the office abruptly swung outward, and Slim appeared on the walk. Slim's hand fisted a short-barreled .45, and he spoke sharply but in low tones to the man waiting with the horses: "All set, Red?"

"All set," answered the man in the saddle.

Slim turned and motioned with his left hand and put his back to Bill as he held open the screen door. Tom Bostwick came out onto the walk and hurried across it, followed by the last of his crewmen. Slim let the screen door slam and had taken barely a stride across the walk when Bill called sharply: "Hold it!"

Tom Bostwick, ducking to step under the tie rail, straightened slowly and faced the passageway. The man holding the horses went rigid in the saddle. Slim's companion stepped in his tracks and hesitated, hands clawed over holsters.

After the first second's hesitation, Slim moved quickly. He spun about, his gun exploding in a stab of powder flame that lined at the mouth of the passageway.

Bill had expected something like this and had

ducked back. As the puff of dust sprayed outward from the corner of the wall nicked by Slim's bullet, Bill moved out and swung his gun into line at his hip. His finger squeezed the trigger. The gun exploded and slapped back against his wrist. He saw Slim's tall shape jerk abruptly backward. Slim's right arm dropped to his side, his fingers opened, and his weapon fell with a *thud* to the planking of the wall. Bringing up his left hand, he clenched his right shoulder and cursed savagely.

Neither the man in the saddle nor the one on the walk made any move to draw guns. Tom Bostwick wasn't carrying one.

After a moment, Bill ordered: "Back you go, Bostwick."

The rancher's big shape seemed to grow visibly smaller. His shoulders lost their square line. He lifted his hands outward in a helpless gesture and said in a strained, harsh voice: "Thanks for tryin' anyway, boys. You'd better get Slim to a doctor."

He crossed the walk toward the door as Bill approached it from the mouth of the passageway. The office was in darkness, and, as the rancher went in through the door, Bill told him: "Light the lamp." He was eyeing Slim and the other pair as he spoke.

Slim's gaunt face was drawn in pain as the light from the lamp Bostwick lit shone abruptly out the window and across the walk. Slim said: "Stranger, you've bought yourself some real trouble as soon as this arm gets back into shape. Don't forget!"

Bill saw that Slim's shirt was stained darkly at the shoulder now. He drawled: "Better do like your boss said, go see a doctor, Slim."

He made a motion with his gun that Slim reluctantly obeyed. The tall man and his companion ducked under the tie rail and climbed into their saddles. As they turned out into the street, Bill heard men running toward him along the walk and turned to see figures spilling from the two saloon doorways. It was the sound of the shot that was bringing them.

He watched Slim and the others ride away, then turned to face the first man to come running toward him. It was Ray Mankey. He was out of breath but managed to get out: "What the hell happened? Where's Ben?"

Bill jerked his head toward the office door. "He's in there. So's Bostwick. His crew tried to break him out. Better get in there while I hold this mob back."

Mankey stepped on past him and in through the jail door. Three men who had followed closely on Mankey's heels broke out of their run to a walk, approaching. Bill called: "Break it up, gents! The sheriff was cleanin' his iron. It went off by accident."

Half a dozen others had come up now and were listening to what Bill said. One of them said truculently: "What were Slim Hall and his crew doin' here?"

"Go ask Slim," Bill answered.

"You're the jasper that brought Bostwick in today, ain't you?" asked another. His tone had a jeering edge to it.

Now better than a dozen men stood closely grouped less than ten feet away along the walk. Bill's glance singled out the last speaker. He drawled: "What about it?" For five long seconds there was an ominous silence. Bill saw that what he had said had made these men hesitate, and now he added sharply: "I said to break it up!"

"I'm stayin'," came the surly words of the man who had asked about Slim.

Bill took one slow stride toward the group. They edged away. He advanced another step. At the back of the group, someone said sharply: "Better come along, Hank!"

That seemed to dictate the rest. They turned and drifted away down the street, one or two taking their time about it, but following the others by the time Bill turned and started back toward the office door.

Bill pulled open the screen and stepped inside. He thought it odd that the lamp on the desk was without its shade. The light was so bright that he had to squint against its glare. In a moment his eyes focused to the glare and what he first saw was the sheriff, lying face down on the floor, hands and arms laced behind him with a piece of rope and a blue bandanna tied about his mouth.

His glance moved to the back of the room. Ray Mankey was standing with his back to the jail door, his hands raised to the level of his shoulders, the holsters at his thighs empty.

Suddenly, to Bill's left, Tom Bostwick's deep voice intoned: "Careful, Brand! Don't move!"

Bill turned his head to see the rancher, standing less than four feet away, between the door and the window. He held a double-barreled Greener leveled squarely at Bill's waist. From the third finger of his left hand dangled two heavy rings of keys, Alcott's and Mankey's keys to the jail.

Bill slowly raised his hands, knowing in that instant that he had made a mistake in letting Bostwick enter the office alone. Above the sheriff's desk was a gun rack. If he'd remembered the rack and the half dozen weapons it held, he wouldn't have sent Bostwick in to light the lamp three minutes ago.

Bostwick said: "Turn around!" Bill turned his back and felt the weight of his gun ease off his right thigh as the rancher took the weapon. "Now over there with Mankey! Ray, pull that door open!"

As Bill moved across to face Mankey, the deputy reached back and pulled the jail door open, saying: "You can't make this stick, Bostwick."

"Watch me," challenged the rancher, prodding Bill from behind with the snout of the shotgun.

Bill stepped into the jail after Mankey. Bostwick's rugged face was set in a tight smile as he looked in at them. "Holler your heads off," he said significantly, nodding to the jail's one small window high on the end wall of the back cell. He swung the door shut to leave them in pitch-black darkness, and they heard the lock to the jail door click shut.

For the space of a long quarter minute neither of them spoke. Finally Ray Mankey let out his breath in

180

a low obscene oath, rasping: "He knew damn' well we can't get at that window! The doors to both them back cells are locked!"

Bill saw the line of light showing beneath the jail door suddenly go out. "What about Alcott?" he asked.

"Didn't you see the way he was roped?" Mankey asked irritably. "He'll stay where he is until someone lets him loose."

Faintly, from out in the street, came the sound of a horse's dust-muffled trot. "That'll be Bostwick on your jughead," Mankey said. He cursed again in impotent rage, saying finally: "Well, do something!"

"Think I'll get some sleep," Bill told him, feeling his way toward the cell Bostwick had occupied. "I'll toss you to see who uses the cot." He took a match from shirt pocket and flicked it alight with his thumbnail. Holding it in one hand, he took out one of the ten-dollar gold pieces the sheriff had given him.

Mankey whistled softly: "Where'd you get that?"

"Alcott gave it to me. Got it out of a money belt in his safe."

Bill didn't understand the look that came to Ray Mankey's face then. It contained surprise and a degree of amusement as the deputy said: "Ben's gettin' mighty generous in his old age, ain't he?" Then the match went out, and, reaching for another, Bill thought that Mankey's peculiar expression had probably been a trick of the wavering feeble light.

When he'd struck the second match, he flipped the

coin in the air, caught it, and slapped it down on the back of his other hand. "Call it," he said.

"Heads."

It was tails. Bill went into the cell and pulled the one blanket from the cot, handing it across to the deputy whose thick-featured face was surly in disappointment. "It may help soften that rock floor," Bill said as Mankey took the blanket.

As he lay back on the cot and stared up into the darkness, thinking back over the day's happenings, he heard Mankey, settling down on the floor nearby. The deputy was muttering angrily under his breath, and once he said aloud: "Wait'll I get my chance at Bostwick."

Bill smiled to himself. "You'd have done the same, Mankey."

His only reply was an irritable snort of anger. Ray Mankey was a poor loser.

V

At five the next morning the sharp clang of a hammer on the steel-faced jail door jerked Bill into abrupt wakefulness. The hammer stroke came again, deafeningly, and in the feeble light from the end cell window Bill saw Mankey wince at the sound and come awake.

"Won't be long now," he said, amused at the deputy's look, puffy-eyed and still angry.

The next two hours proved Bill wrong, for the explosive metallic hammering on the door continued at rarely broken intervals. Later, they learned that the blacksmith Ben Alcott had brought in to break the lock on the door had dulled seven cold chisels against the hardened steel before it gave way under his blows.

When the door finally swung open on squeaking hinges, Ben Alcott stepped in. The spaniel-like expression was gone from his brown eyes now. They were red-rimmed and glinted coldly in a way that Bill had never seen. His face looked old and ugly in a frown. When he saw the purple-angry expression on Ray Mankey's face, he laughed mirthlessly and held out his hands. The skin along his wrists was rubbed nearly raw.

"You think you had a tough time! How about me?" he said. "Took me until four o'clock to break loose from Slim Hall's hog-tyin'." His glance went to Bill and some of the flintiness went out of his eyes. "Looks like I'm havin' a hard time gettin' rid of you, Brand. Thanks for makin' the try last night. Slim's got a busted shoulder. Aside from that, we didn't do ourselves much good."

"What happened to the keys?" Mankey asked.

The sheriff laughed. "I reckon Tom Bostwick's keepin' 'em to remember us by."

Bill said: "I'd like another try at Bostwick, Sheriff."

"You're gettin' one," Alcott told him. "Tonight."

Interest flared alive across Ray Mankey's face. "What's the play, boss?"

"The bank's takin' out eviction papers on Bostwick today, in case his note isn't paid up." A significant look of understanding passed between Alcott and his deputy. "It's up to us to serve 'em. We'll wait until midnight and move in on him."

"See if you can find him," Mankey said.

"He'll be there, at his lay-out. He's too bull-headed to hide anywhere else. We'll take him and kick the crew off the place, all at the same time. I'll deputize a dozen men and blast him out of there if he turns any guns on us!"

Bill saw that the sheriff was too angry this morning to reason in his usual logical way. He said mildly: "What's the matter with just the three of us doin' it?"

"Bostwick will fight," the lawman insisted doggedly. "I'm through foolin' with him. Breaking jail's a serious offense."

Bill nodded. "But Bostwick has friends. Shoot up his lay-out and his crew and you'll stand about as much chance on your next election as the mouse that overslept in the meat grinder."

The mildness of his tone along with the logic of his argument wiped out the last of Ben Alcott's unreasoning anger. The sheriff said: "Understand one thing, Brand. You ain't obliged to stay."

Bill said: "I'll stay."

"What's your idea on how we ought to do this?"

Bill told them.

Tom Bostwick knew he was licked at four that afternoon, closing time for the bank. But he didn't admit it to himself until shortly after dark, when Red Short rode in from the mesa rim where all afternoon he'd been watching for the sign of a rider coming in off the desert out of the direction Bill Duncan should have come.

Red came into the main room of the house at dusk, as the rancher and his daughter were eating their evening meal. He took his hat off as he opened the door, caught Bostwick's eye, and shook his head in the silent signal that was the blasting of the last of the rancher's forlorn hopes.

A long-running sigh escaped Bostwick's broad chest. "Better go out to the cook shack and get something to eat, Red," he said.

"I ain't hungry, boss. Give me something to do."

"You might gather up all the guns in the bunkhouse and bring 'em in here," Bostwick told him.

"Dad, you're not going through with this!" Ann cried, turning in her chair to face the door. "Red, don't do it!"

"I reckon I am," the rancher stated, adding tersely: "Go ahead, Red."

He waited until his crewman had gone out the door, then gave Ann a long, pleading look as he said: "I've got to, Sis. I wasn't made to give up all this to the first man who tells me to move out."

He looked around the room. It was large, high-ceilinged, furnished with things Tom Bostwick had taken half his life to collect, priceless old Navajo rugs, crude yet beautiful furniture that had been shaped by hand by the first Spanish settlers of this vast region a century ago. The table at which he and Ann sat was one solid slab pegged to sturdy carved legs. Its top surface was uneven, showing the axe marks of the craftsman who had hewn it from the three-foot trunk of a pine. The cherry wood sofa that sat near the huge stone fireplace at the end of the room had been hauled to Santa Fé overland by a team of oxen, and from there to this frontier by mule team. The pewter service on the high sideboard had been sailed by packet from England, around the Horn and to San Francisco back in the early days of the gold rush of 1849. Tom Bostwick had made his start as a boy in his teens in California during those days and had bought the pewter at a store in San Francisco when his pockets had been heavy with gold. The pewter was a gift to the girl he hoped someday to ask to be his wife. She'd brought it with her when they had come into this country.

Ann seemed to understand that glance of her father's that slowly traveled the room. She said in a humble voice: "I know, Dad. But you can't fight the law."

Grim determination corded the muscles along Bostwick's square jaw. "You'd better get your things packed, Sis," he said. "I'll get Red to drive you to town. Alcott's no fool. He won't come after me until past midnight, until my chance of payin' up on the note has run out. But he'll come then. I don't want you around when it happens."

"I'm not going," Ann said in a hushed voice.

Bostwick seemed to sense that there was nothing he could say to put down this stubborn rebellion in her.

Because she had always implicitly obeyed his every wish, her refusal now was all the more pointed.

He seemed to accept her refusal, for he got up out of the chair, saying: "I'd better get everything set. There's only four hours to go."

He turned from the table and took a short-stemmed briar pipe from his pocket and was sifting tobacco from a pouch into the bowl when his glance happened to go toward the door where Red had stood a few moments ago. His hands stopped moving, and his fingers went limp. The pipe fell to the floor.

Bill Duncan was leaning indolently against the smooth adobe wall to one side of the door. He wore a deputy sheriff's badge on the pocket of his vest. There was a tight smile on his square face, and his hands hung by the thumbs from the belt of his single holster.

He slowly moved his head in a negative way, saying: "You're too late, Bostwick."

Ann was sitting with her back to the door. At the sound of his voice, she gasped audibly and turned quickly in her chair. Her face drained of color, and her mouth opened to speak. But she couldn't summon her voice.

Tom Bostwick stood motionless for three seconds, letting his defeat sink in on him. A gathering rage made itself plain on his face. All at once his glance swung away from Bill and to the near corner of the room where a Winchester leaned against the wall. His big frame gathered in a sudden lunge toward the rifle.

Bill had seen that glance and the object of it. When

he saw what Bostwick intended, he eased out from the wall. As the rancher moved, Bill moved with him. Four steps put him within reach of the rifle. He snatched it up, sidestepped Bostwick's rush, and backed away, levering the Winchester's magazine empty as he moved. He dropped the shells into his pocket, and then tossed the weapon onto the broad couch right-angled out from the big stone fireplace.

He said: "Be good, Bostwick. There's nothin' you can do about it."

The scraping of boots against the hard-packed earth sounded from outside, and in another moment Ben Alcott's voice called a muted shout: "Open up, Brand!"

Bill went to the door and threw it open, stepping back out of the way as seven men filed into the room. Slim Hall came first, his face set in dogged anger and his right arm hanging in a flour-sack sling. Red came next, then two other crewmen followed by the cook who had evidently been caught at his after-supper dishwashing, for he wore a splashed apron, and the hair along his thick arms was powdery with dried soap.

Ben Alcott and Ray Mankey brought up the rear. Both carried guns in their hands, and Mankey had half a dozen others slung over his shoulder by a length of rope he'd run through the trigger guards.

As the sheriff backed into the door to shut it, he drawled: "'Evenin', Tom. You might as well all sit and be comfortable. We're doin' this up accordin' to law, so we'll wait until midnight and give this Bill Duncan a chance to turn up with the money."

Tom Bostwick's deep-toned voice rumbled: "I'm a fool, or I'd have found you out twenty years ago, Alcott!"

The sheriff's face assumed a hurt yet somehow benign expression. "I hate this as bad as you do, Tom. But I reckon you are a fool. Otherwise you'd have acted different in the beginnin'. You resisted arrest, you broke jail, and now you. . . ."

"You're a damned paid understrapper for a stinkin' sheep outfit!" Bostwick cut in with a roar. "You're. . . ."

Ann spoke for the first time since these men had entered the room, sharply, in a tone that cut short her father's outburst: "Dad! Don't! It isn't the sheriff's fault!"

"Then whose is it?" Bostwick snapped.

Bill's even drawl answered him. "No one's, Bostwick. Chalk it up to hard luck."

Bostwick turned on him, his anger controlled now but still a deep-running and consuming passion. "Who asked you to buy into this, Brand? And what the hell do you know about it?" He seemed to realize the saltiness of his language for the first time, for he gave Ann a half-apologetic glance, and, when he went on, his voice was quieter. "I've been framed with murder. The bank's framed me with a foreclosure when they're extending the notes of a dozen other outfits in worse shape than mine. What does it add up to? It adds up to John Alcott's making a nice piece of change by selling out this range to sheep! Ben, you're in with him on it!"

"You don't know what you're sayin', Tom," the lawman remarked in a grieved tone.

There was a brief silence, broken finally by Slim whose glance had remained fixed on Bill. He said flatly: "Come to think of it, I won't need to wait till this arm's healed. Unless you're jailin' me, Sheriff, I'm choosin' your new deputy the first time I get my hands on an iron."

Ben Alcott said: "Take it easy, Slim. You aren't bein' jailed, and you're not choosin' anyone." He glanced at the girl and added courteously: "You'd better pack your things, Ann. Brand, you go along and help her."

"I don't need his help!" Ann flared.

"Then he can go along and watch," Ben said in sudden impatience.

"Let her go alone, Sheriff," Bill said.

Ann gave him a grateful look, then glanced at her father. Tom Bostwick seemed to be realizing finally that nothing he could do would prevent this catastrophe from overtaking him. He sat down heavily in his chair at the table. Ann rose, put her hand on his shoulder in a gesture that was meant to be reassuring, and then crossed the room and went down the hallway to her room.

Alone, she gave way to her grief. For nearly a quarter hour she lay face down on her bed, letting the tears come and feeling better when she had cried it out. Then, resolutely, she set about a task that was the hardest she'd ever attempted—the packing of

190

her things. It was hard because she knew that never again would this room hold for her the rich memories of a happy life. The room seemed to have lost something. Each ornament, each treasured thing in it now seemed lifeless and the memories they held were empty of the deep flavor they'd once held. In the end, she took only the clothes she knew she'd need in the next few days, leaving everything else behind.

Presently she finished putting her things into a fiber telescope suitcase and went across to her father's room to pack his things. It was almost more than she could stand, sorting through his clothes and finally trying to pack into his big brassbound trunk the relics of his full life. Going through his desk was hardest. In the top drawer she found the daguerreotype of her mother. A San Francisco photographer's name was engraved on the frame, along with the date. Her mother had been only nineteen then, and the beautiful cameo-like face staring up at her out of the brownish tones of the picture seemed to have a new and tragic look, as though that girl had known that her flesh and blood would one day be dragged into the depths of despair.

It was done, finally, and she went back into her own room to wait out the hours until midnight. For a time she restlessly walked the floor, trying to see some way out for her father. Then, giving up, she lay on the bed and closed her eyes. Merciful sleep wiped out her torment of thought.

The two hours before midnight dragged endlessly for Bill. No one talked, and the girl didn't come back into the room. The sheriff told Mankey to take the crew, one by one, to the bunkhouse to pack their belongings. The deputy's several trips outside were finally finished, the crew's war bags and blanket rolls piled up inside the door. Then there was only waiting, with each man in the room seeming to watch the clock on the mantel of the fireplace. Its hands circled with unbearable slowness. Once Tom Bostwick said— "Let's go in to town and end this nonsense!"—but Ben Alcott shook his head and answered: "No. I'm doin' this my way. We'll wait." After that, the ticking of the clock became loud in the stillness.

Finally the clock's twelve chiming strokes ended their waiting. The door to the hall opened, and Ann walked into the room. Tom Bostwick pushed himself up out of the chair and said flatly: "You've won, Sheriff."

Ben Alcott shook his head. "Not me, Tom. I didn't want to do this." He motioned to Mankey to open the door, and they all filed out, the crew carrying their outfits, Tom Bostwick empty-handed.

In the yard, Alcott said: "Better hitch up a buckboard for yourself and Ann, Tom." He nodded to Bill and added: "You can be bringin' their stuff out, Brand."

Ten minutes later, when Tom Bostwick drove the buckboard close to the front door, Bill was waiting with the trunk and Ann's suitcase. He lifted them into the buckboard's shallow bed. The crew rode up from the corral, with Ben Alcott and Mankey bringing up the rear. No word was spoken as Tom Bostwick reached down to take his daughter's hand and help her climb to the seat beside him.

Ben Alcott called: "Brand, you stay here and watch things! I'll send Ray out to spell you in the mornin'."

Bostwick lifted his reins and slapped the backs of the team of bays. The rig rattled out of sight in the darkness along the lane, and the crew strung out behind, Mankey and the sheriff still hanging at the rear. Bill's last glimpse of the girl showed him her face for a fleeting instant as she turned to take a parting look at the house. Then her head turned away and lowered, and that gesture was so symbolical of what was taking place that Bill felt a momentary self-loathing. He had helped to do this, helped seal the circumstance of misfortune that was dragging a strong man down. He wasn't proud of it.

He wondered what he ought to do now. Because he was restless and wide-awake, he walked through the lay-out—barn, wagon shed, blacksmith shop, cook shanty, and finally down to the corrals. Someone had thought to leave the pole gates down, and half a dozen head of horses were drifting aimlessly away toward the pasture as Bill came up. Whoever had done that had seemed to accept the fact that no one would be here to look after the animals from now on. The lay-out seemed empty of all life, and later, in the bunkhouse, Bill was touched by the deserted look of things.

On the sill of one bunkhouse window he found the cracked shard of a mirror, a piece of silvered glass some man had doubtless used until tonight but had thought too worthless to take along. That piece of mirror was the only sign of occupancy, the only evidence that men's hearty laughter and salty language had once filled the narrow confines of this bunk-lined room. There were no blankets on the bunks, and their faded and thin cotton mattresses had a bare look that made him glad to turn away finally and walk out into the chill and bracing night air. In there he had felt like an intruder.

He went back to the house. But, opening the door, he experienced again the feeling that he had no right here, that the house's stillness was in some way unfriendly and accusing. He shut the door and sat outside on the doorstep. Tied to a low picket fence that ringed a huge cottonwood forty feet out in the yard, his white-stockinged black horse, loaned by Ray Mankey, now and then stamped nervously, seeming to feel the same unfriendly quality to his surroundings that Bill had noticed.

It was while he was sitting there that the bullet-gash along the side of his head set up a dull, throbbing ache. The pain increased to a tormenting intensity. A spell of dizziness hit him so violently that he had to reach down and steady himself with both palms placed flatly against the ground. Sweat beaded his forehead and ran down his face, even though the air was chill and penetrating. That time of pain engulfed him for almost two minutes. He wanted to cry out against it but couldn't summon the strength.

A nausea gripped him. His mind shaped a maze of clear-patterned images. There was a fire's bright light cutting the gloom of darkness beside a pond of still water that reflected the light of the flames. A frying pan simmered on the fire, and he could catch the clear fragrance of boiling coffee. Sitting there, he imagined himself as moving across the fire and stooping to take something from the pouch of a saddle that had a strangely familiar feel under the touch of his hand. He came back to the fire and squatted alongside it, staring bleakly into the red coals. Then, sharply, a stunning blow struck him on the head, and he was falling . . . falling. . . .

Objects before his eyes settled slowly out of the gyrating whirl of his temporary blindness. There was the cottonwood's white picket enclosure, and there stood the black with white-stockinged forelegs, Ray Mankey's horse. Here, solidly under him, was the doorstep. The pain in his head was gone now, as completely as were the images his mind had shaped during the past minute.

He straightened and mopped his damp face with his bandanna, whistling softly as he let his breath out and muttered aloud: "You're seein' things!"

He tried to bring back the clear pictures his mind had shaped. But now they became confused and without meaning. Once or twice a flash of clarity would return, and it seemed as though he was on the verge of making some vital discovery. He tried hard to pin it down, to force his mind to jump the last hurdle between obscurity and understanding. Then, gradually, all sense and order left his imaginings, and in the end he could recall no single detail of them, not even a general idea of what they had been.

He swore calmly and stood up and built a smoke. He took off his Stetson and felt gingerly of the bandage above his temple. The soreness was almost gone. All at once, filled with impatience and a little anger over not being able to remember what was in his mind during that torturing long interval of pain, he took one corner of the bandage and ripped it off, wincing as the sticking plaster stuck to his hair. He tossed the bandage aside and felt the cool air strike against the tender flesh of the healing gash. It felt better without the bandage.

He was standing there, still vainly trying to grope back and catch some significance in what had happened, when he heard a far-off sound that brought his stocky body tense in a listening attitude. The sound shuttled softly across the night air, a low drone he couldn't quite define. For five minutes he stood there listening, and during that interval the sound increased minutely. Finally he distinguished above the lower tones one that was higher-pitched. It was a faint, prolonged blasting, as though a baby lay crying in its crib almost at the limits of his hearing.

Suddenly he knew what it was, although his forget-fulness of the past couldn't tell him how he knew. He was hearing sheep on the move, not a few but a horde of the animals, and now he imagined he could catch the faint, pungent odor of their shaggy hides tainting the cool clear air. A grimace of disgust crossed his face. Then anger rode in on him in a blinding wave. He threw his cigarette into the dust and ground it under the heel of his boot. In sudden decision he started out toward his horse.

He was standing at the picket fence when he heard the muffled hoof thuds of a walking horse coming from the direction of the corrals. The black's head came up, and Bill's hand instinctively reached out and clamped about the animal's nostrils, choking back his whicker. Shortly, out of the night's obscurity, walked a horse with a rider's thick shape in the saddle.

Bill stayed where he was, waiting warily with his right arm rigid. The rider came on. In a few more moments Bill saw that the man wasn't looking at him but in toward the darkened windows of the house. Then he was close enough so that Bill could see the Winchester cradled across the saddle horn.

The rider drew rein less than thirty feet away. His attitude seemed one of listening, one of wariness. For five long seconds he sat there unmoving. Then his hands lifted the reins, and his horse started turning back in the direction out of which he had come.

Bill called softly: "Lookin' for someone?"

At the instant he spoke, he let go his hold on the

horse's snout and palmed the heavy Colt from his holster and swung it into line.

His words made the rider face around sharply. The Winchester's barrel swung around, but not completely, for the man saw the gun in Bill's hand and was warned by it.

"*¡Buenas noches, señor!*" said the rider in a voice that grated with a mixture of deference and fear. His frame seemed to relax then, and his rifle's barrel lowered. He turned his horse and brought the animal on half a dozen strides, to within ten feet of where Bill stood.

Bill kept his weapon lined. "Sing out. Who are you?"

"Seferino Gallegos, they call me." The rider reached up and swept his overly wide sombrero from his head in a generous flourish. "I bring my sheep, *señor*."

"What sheep?"

"The sheep *Señor* Alcott he tell me to bring."

VI

Sheer surprise and bewilderment held Bill wordless for a five second interval. Then the anger of a minute ago flared up in him once more. Four strides put him alongside the Mexican's tapaderoed stirrup, and he coaxed: "Say that again."

His tone had an edge to it that wiped the genial smile from the Mexican's dark face. Its expression showed genuine fear in the faint starlight.

Bill snapped: "You're drivin' sheep in? The sheriff ordered you to?"

The Mexican's head tilted sharply in a quick nod.

"You lie!" Bill said.

Suddenly he reached up and took a hold on the man's shirt front and threw all his weight against the arm. Seferino Gallegos slid unresisting from the saddle, dropping the rifle and almost falling to his knees against the pull of Bill's arm as his boots touched the ground. Abruptly he was whirled to face Bill squarely.

"Out with it!" Bill's voice said harshly. "Who's bringin' those sheep in?"

"Me, *señor*, I bring the sheep! I do what they tell me!"

"And what did they tell you?"

"To cut the wire at midnight! To drive my sheep into the pasture! She's the truth, *señor!* I swear it by *san.* . . ."

"To hell with that! Who ordered you to drive your stinkin' mess into this range?"

"*Señor* Alcott."

"Ben Alcott?"

"No. His brother."

"John Alcott?"

Gallegos swallowed with difficulty, as though his throat was dry with cotton. He nodded.

"What about the sheriff?"

Gallegos's shoulders lifted, and he spread his hands in an unknowing gesture.

Bill shook him. "Are you here on the sheriff's orders?"

"I know nothing, *señor*. Tonight, a man come out from town to my camp. He give me paper from *Señor* Alcott. Me, I no read. I ask him to tell me what the paper say. He say what I tell you. I am to drive sheep through fence at midnight."

Bill thought he understood now. Ben Alcott, honest to the core, had done his sworn duty in serving an eviction notice on Tom Bostwick. But in clearing Wagon Fork's crew off the lay-out, the sheriff had played into the hands of a dishonest brother. John Alcott was now clearly to blame for Tom Bostwick's trouble. The Bill Duncan who had promised to be on his way with the money had unaccountably failed to arrive, and now the sheep were on their way in. The Wagon Fork, as a cattle outfit, was doomed.

Bill released his hold on the Mexican's shirt front, asking sharply: "How many men are working that drive?"

"Miguel, Victorino, Maclovio, Porfirio, me."

"How many sheep?"

"Two, t'ree t'ousan' head."

Bill noticed then the holster at the Mexican's wrist. Gallegos wore his gun high at his belt, butt foremost for a cross-draw. Bill reached out and took the weapon, ramming it through the waist band of his Levi's as he stated: "You want to go to jail, to the *jusgado*, Gallegos?"

A frightened look crossed the Mexican's swarthy face. "No, *señor!* *¡Mi Dios!*"

"See this?" Bill indicated the badge pinned to the pocket of his vest.

Gallegos's glance dropped, and his fright was written plainly on his face now. He gulped and said: "I see it, *señor*."

"You're going to drive those sheep back through the fence."

Gallegos nodded reluctantly. "You say so, me do anything."

"You're to tell the rest that! They're to help you, or I take them to jail."

"But *señor*. . . ."

"You'll start now," Bill cut in. "I'll go with you."

"My boss, he give me hell!"

"But your boss can't put you in jail. I can."

"*Sí, señor*." Gallegos turned toward his horse.

Bill followed him closely as he left the lay-out. The sound of the oncoming sheep was louder now. Gallegos's men were driving them deep into Wagon Fork's pasture. Presently, when they'd ridden better than a mile south and east, Bill and the Mexican came upon the herd, a gray and slow-moving mass of animals that advanced across the lush grass meadow. They saw two riders in the obscure night shadows off to the left, and Gallegos swung across there and rode up on them.

He spoke in Spanish to his two men. Bill was surprised to find that he understood what was said, although in these last two days, since losing his memory, he'd had no occasion to be reminded of that. Gallegos was badly frightened and volubly told his men of meeting the *gringo* deputy, of being ordered out on the threat of being jailed if he disobeyed. At first the pair that listened to his story gave Bill sultry, hostile looks, but then, impressed by the severity of the threatened punishment, they seemed to feel a little of the fear that was gripping their foreman.

Shortly Gallegos sent one of the pair across to the other side of the herd to tell the others. He and the remaining man rode to the head of the thick column of sheep and started them swinging around, Bill following and watching their movements. Bill stayed at the point of the herd, occasionally swinging out to turn back animals that tried to break from the main body. Gallegos disappeared into the darkness, and Bill worked with the remaining crewman.

An hour and a quarter later they reached the fence. The four strands of wire between three of the posts were down. Bill reined aside and rode back out of the dust to watch the herd go out. Presently Gallegos rode up out of the darkness and reined alongside, wiping the dust from his black face, and his dark eyes showed a look of concern.

"*Amigo*, you explain to *Señor* Alcott?" he asked worriedly.

"Sure," Bill drawled. "Have your men string that wire again."

Gallegos nodded, and rode on down to the break. It

was forty minutes before the last of the sheep were pushed through the fence, another twenty before Gallegos and one of his men had succeeded in mending the wire and tightening it. They rode away without looking back at Bill again.

Bill stayed there until the sound of the sheep herd had nearly died out in the distance. Then, drawing the Mexican's gun from his belt, he tossed it across the fence, and rode on back to the lay-out. He was tired now, and, as he went in through the door to Tom Bostwick's room, a last look at the wheeling stars in the dark void of the heavens told him that it was past three. He crossed the darkened room and lay down on the bed. Two minutes later he was asleep.

The closing of the hall door four hours later jerked him into sudden wakefulness. He opened his eyes to see Ray Mankey, standing just inside the door. Mankey's blunt face was set in a dark scowl of obvious dislike as he looked toward the bed. Bill lay unmoving, eyes half closed, trying to read that look. Then, abruptly, he opened his eyes and sat up. Mankey was smiling.

"Wondered where you were," Mankey said genially. "Everything OK?"

"Everything but that bunch of sheep I had to chase out an hour after you left last night," Bill said.

Mankey frowned seriously. "Sheep?" he echoed, his tone not quite convincing.

Bill nodded.

"How come?" Mankey asked.

"They said the bank had ordered them to drive in here after midnight."

Mankey swore, his look going ugly. "How the hell could that be?"

"The bank ordered them in."

Mankey let out one explosive obscene oath, then shrugged and let his breath out in a gusty sigh. "If John Alcott sent 'em, I reckon there's nothin' we can do about it. He'll make it stick."

"What'll Ben say?"

"He'll be sore, like we are. But Ben can't stop the bank, if they want to sell the lay-out to that sheep outfit."

Bill's eyes narrowed. Suddenly he shot a question, remembering the deputy's look on entering the room: "What do you know about this, Mankey?"

"Me? Nothin'."

"You didn't know sheep were comin' in?"

"Not for sure. I had a hunch they might."

Bill decided then that he'd get nothing from Mankey, although he was sure that the man knew something. That one look, when Mankey had thought him asleep and been caught off guard, would bear some explaining. He meant to find out what was in back of it.

He got up off the bed, clamped his Stetson on his head, and said: "I'll head for town and break the news to the sheriff."

"Yeah, he ought to know about it," Mankey said noncommittally.

"Bostwick's crew sore?"

Mankey grinned. "They ain't happy about bein' kicked out. Slim's the worst. He don't love you much, Brand. Ben put 'em all under peace bonds, just in case they get any fancy ideas. Bostwick put up the *dinero*."

"Where's Bostwick?"

"Jail."

"How about the girl?"

Mankey's look became a smug one. "Nice, ain't she?" A warning look that came to Bill's eyes made him add hastily: "She's puttin' up at the hotel."

"What about all the stuff they left behind, the furniture and what's in the sheds?"

"Ben's takin' care of that. They get their personal belongin's but nothin' else. I reckon there'll be an auction out here in a week or so. If there's anything left after the bank's paid off, Bostwick gets it."

Bill felt again the same self-loathing as last night, the same impotent anger at the realization that it was his idea that had succeeded in putting Tom Bostwick and his daughter off the place. He said savagely, on the impulse of the moment: "This whole thing stinks, Mankey!"

"Don't I know it!"

"What kind of a man is this John Alcott? What made him call Bostwick's note?"

Mankey shrugged his heavy shoulders. "I ain't no banker, friend. I wouldn't know."

Bill gave the deputy a long, level look, drawling finally: "I wonder."

"Wonder what?"

Bill didn't reply for a brief moment. Then he said: "Nothin'. I was thinkin' out loud."

Later, where the trail took to the margin of the trees far out across the pasture, Bill brought the black gelding to a stand and spent a long quarter minute looking back toward the lay-out, still trying to grasp some meaning from the look Mankey had given him on entering the room half an hour ago. He wasn't at all sure that the look had meant anything but an instinctive dislike the deputy might feel for him. But neither was he sure now that Mankey was ignorant of the reasons behind that sheep drive in the early morning hours.

It was while he sat there, looking out across the pasture, that he saw a rider come out of the trees along the lane before the house and cut obliquely east across the pasture. Bill recognized the bay horse of Ray Mankey's that he'd seen tied to the picket fence around the cottonwood in the yard before the house a few minutes ago.

Curiosity came up strongly in Bill as he saw that Mankey seemed to be in a hurry, for now the bay had broken into a mile-eating lope. That curiosity gave way to a suspicion that an urgent errand was taking Mankey out across the pasture toward the spot where the sheep-herders had last night cut Wagon Fork's fence. Perhaps Mankey was only checking on Bill's story of the cut fence. But why should he doubt Bill's word?

206

Almost before he had defined the impulse of not trusting Mankey, Bill reined his black around and left the trail, following a line that paralleled the one the deputy was taking. While Mankey was in sight, he kept well within the edge of the timber. Then, when a low knoll hid the deputy from sight, he rode out into the meadow and lifted the black to a run. When he rounded the edge of the low rise, he was closer to the bay horse, and far out across the pasture he could see the swath of grass that had been trampled by the sheep herd last night. Here he struck back into the trees again.

Time and again the indented line of the timber would take him out of sight of the pasture, down into shallow gullies or behind low hills that edged the mesa rim. But occasionally he rode into sight of it, and once he had a far look at Mankey who was riding in on Wagon Fork's east fence at almost the exact spot where the wire had been cut.

Mankey was better than a mile away when Bill caught that last glimpse of him. Instinctively Bill kept to the trees, going slower now, and picking his way carefully, warily, not bothering to reason out his thought that he should keep out of sight.

He didn't come within sight of the fence again for twenty minutes, for the timber made a wide half circle to the south, and he rode better than three miles in covering the direct line of the mile to the fence. Halfway there, he heard again the sounds he'd heard last night, the distant mutter of sheep on the move, the incessant bleating that grew louder each moment.

Topping the crest of a rise a quarter of a mile from the fence, Bill came suddenly within sight of a moving mass of sheep. They were pouring through the line of the fence. The wire was down in the same place it had been cut last night. He saw Gallegos riding point with another man. The Mexican had another rifle, and again he carried his weapon in readiness, cradled across the horn of his saddle.

Bill understood what lay behind this in an instant. Mankey's look back there in Tom Bostwick's room had meant something, after all. Mankey's job this morning had been to get rid of Bill and then ride across here to signal the sheep crew to begin their drive through Wagon Fork's fence once again. Sometime this morning one of Gallegos's men must have carried the news into town, the news that Ben Alcott's new deputy had turned the herd back last night. New arrangements had been made, and Ray Mankey was in on them.

Bill didn't see Mankey again in the quarter hour he sat there, watching the herd spreading out across the pasture. The deputy was probably back along the herd somewhere, urging the men to hurry. Bill didn't wait to see how many sheep were moving in before he started back toward the trail that would take him to town. He'd seen enough to be able to tell Ben Alcott how thoroughly he was being double-crossed by his deputy.

VII

Ben Alcott was tired and irritable that morning, unaccustomed as he was to losing two nights' sleep in a row. He'd turned in at two last night, with Tom Bostwick safe in jail and Wagon Fork's crew sullen under the threat of their peace bonds. He'd expected to get some sleep.

At four-thirty John Alcott had come up to his hotel room with the news of Bill's turning back the sheep. The banker was worried and afraid, and wanted to back out on his part in the sheep deal. It had taken Ben a full hour of arguments, threats, and careful reasoning to bring back John's nerve. At the end of that hour it was broad daylight, and the sheriff couldn't go back to sleep.

He'd had four cups of coffee at six, two more at eight, and now, at ten, he was leaving the Elite Café with three more under his belt when he looked up the street to see Bill, riding in off the trail at the far end. His grizzled face took on a belligerent frown as he eyed his new deputy. He was thinking that today he'd have to get rid of Bill for good. He thought he knew how to set about doing it, and started along the awninged walk toward his jail office.

As he came abreast the front of the Peacock saloon, the swing doors opened outward and Slim Hall stepped out, asking: "Have any bad dreams last night, Sheriff?"

Ben stopped, gave Slim a long measuring look, and answered: "I never dream."

"Your conscience don't bother you?" Slim asked blandly.

Behind him, Red Short and another Wagon Fork man shouldered out the doors. The glances they fixed on the lawman were plainly unfriendly, almost threatening. Slim's wasn't exactly hostile; instead, it was mocking. Slim had a narrow and aquiline face that was unreadable even in his easiest moods, and now it betrayed nothing to back the faint amusement in his gray eyes.

"Why should it?" Ben asked.

Slim ignored that. His thin nose wrinkled slightly, and he sniffed, then turned to the pair behind: "Smell anything?" he asked.

"Sheep," Red said with a perfectly straight face. He was a big, raw-boned man and almost as tall as Slim. He looked ready for trouble.

Ben's jaw muscles corded, and anger hardened the look in his eyes. "What the hell are you tryin' to say?"

Slim replied: "Nothin', Sheriff. Can we help it how you stink?"

He stood there, tall, sober, his useless right arm hanging in its sling and his clenched left fist the only sign that betrayed the ready anger in him. His glance didn't soften nor did the glances of the other two.

Ben Alcott, for once, was at a loss for words. His face darkened, and once he opened his mouth to say something, then snapped it shut. He turned, and strode away. There was no sound behind him, but he felt the glances of the trio boring accusingly into his back.

His ugly mood hadn't left him as he jerked open the screen door to his office. Bill was sitting in a chair, tilted back against the wall alongside the desk. Beyond him the jail door was propped shut by a chair with the back wedged under the broken lock. As Alcott entered, Bill announced: "They've moved in."

"Who's moved in where?" the lawman snapped irritably.

"Sheep. Onto Bostwick's place."

Ben Alcott frowned and asked cautiously: "Who says they have?"

"I do. They started in last night. I made the crew drive 'em out. This morning they're back again."

Ben's calculations hadn't included Bill's knowing anything about the sheep being moved in again this morning. Accustomed as he was to hiding his thoughts, he couldn't quite hide his irritation at this new development. Mankey had fallen down on the job, and the lawman inwardly cursed him. But instantly that angry expression was masked before one of mock surprise and indignation. He swore, feelingly, and said: "You sure about this?"

Bill nodded. "Something else," he said. "Ray Mankey's the one who rode across and brought 'em in."

Wariness edged into Ben Alcott's eyes. He wasn't sure of his ground now. After a moment's thought, he blazed explosively: "Mankey?"

"Mankey. He's double-crossin' you, Sheriff."

That statement made Ben a little more sure of how Bill stood on this. As yet there was nothing directly accusing in Bill's words or his look. Ben breathed an oath and said: "Mankey never was worth a damn!"

Bill remained silent for a long moment. Then: "What're you goin' to do about it?"

"What the hell can I do? The sheep are there, aren't they?"

"Are you going to let your brother get away with it?"

"No, by God!" the lawman exploded indignantly. He knew now what he would do to cover up his own guilt. He wheeled toward the door, saying curtly: "Come along!"

On the walk, Bill fell in alongside him, asking: "Where to?"

"The bank."

They went on in silence. Across from the hotel they turned in at the plate glass doors of Rawhide's most pretentious building. The bank was of brick, single-storied but with a high brick false front across which big gilt letters proclaimed: CATTLEMAN'S BANK AND TRUST COMPANY.

Bill followed the lawman on back along the room, past the wickets of the tellers' cages and along a counter to its far end. There, a clerk said politely: " 'Morning, Sheriff. Anything I can do for you?"

Ben pushed through a gate at the counter's end, shoved the man aside without answering, and strode toward a door whose frosted-glass panel was lettered: PRESIDENT. Bill followed.

The lawman's thrust pushed the door open so hard that it banged against the inside wall of John Alcott's office. The banker was standing at a back window that looked out onto the alley. His back was turned, his hands were clasped behind him, and he was chewing the soggy end of a dead cigar.

He wheeled around at the sound of the door's opening. When he saw who it was, his eyes widened, and he reached for the cigar and opened his mouth to say something. Ben's rasping voice cut him off: "What's the meaning of this, John?"

"The meaning of what?" John Alcott managed to get out. He was looking squarely at his brother, plainly afraid. Then he caught the furtive droop of Ben's right eyelid. That wink gave him back some of his nerve.

"Those damned sheep!" Ben snapped. "Sheep on Tom Bostwick's graze!"

Bill had closed the door and was now leaning back against it. John Alcott looked at him, then at his brother. He said finally, in reserved tones: "It's business, Ben. We gave Bostwick his legal notice. We regret having to foreclose on him."

"But, hell, John! Sheep! This is cattle country!"

"Gettin' too dry for cattle," the banker said suavely. "I've approached several cattlemen, but none of them wanted the place. After all, it's up to me to look out for the bank's interest. The Phoenix Sheep Company agreed to meet my figure."

213

Ben seemed to lose hold on his temper. He swore, not once but in a long string of strong oaths. "What figure? I'll lay you a bet the bank's makin a three hundred percent profit!"

His statement seemed to startle John Alcott. But once again the banker caught his brother's meaningful wink and said in reserved tones: "You can see the papers if you want. Bostwick's note was for five thousand. We're selling for sixty-five hundred, which leaves something like nine hundred dollars when court costs and commissions are deducted. We'll turn that nine hundred over to Tom Bostwick." He bent over and opened a drawer of the desk, taking out a folded legal document that he handed the sheriff.

Ben said: "Sixty-five hundred! The Wagon Fork's worth three times that!"

The banker nodded. "In good times, yes. But not now, with money as scarce as it is. We'd like to hold the place and operate it ourselves until we can get a better market. But we can't afford to. Bostwick will have to take his losses."

Ben's face was dark now in an apoplectic flush. He seemed to be hunting for something to say, but in the end he examined the papers his brother had given him, finally turning and holding them out to Bill, saying: "It's down here in black and white."

Before Bill could reach out, he wheeled again toward the banker's desk, throwing the papers on the green blotter and saying savagely: "That's not the point, John! Turn Bostwick's place over to sheep and you'll have every outfit within twenty miles of the Wagon Fork movin' out on you. You carry their notes. They'll let their places go, get out. First thing you know, the bank'll own all that hill graze. Then what're you goin' to do?"

"We'll do the best we can. We may lose some money."

"Why . . . ?" Ben began, then threw his hands palms outward in a gesture that was intended to show his feeling of utter helplessness at further argument.

Bill said: "The sheriff's right, Alcott. Whenever sheep come into a country to stay, cattle move out."

John Alcott said haughtily: "I profess to know something about this range country, stranger. When I want advice, I'll ask for it."

"You will, eh?" Ben blazed out. "John, this is a sell-out! A stinkin' rotten double-cross on your friends! Brand, here, says Ray Mankey's tied up in this. How much are you payin' him? How much did you pay him to bushwhack that sheepherder and frame Tom Bostwick with it?" He paused a moment, not allowing the banker to speak as he went on: "I'm lettin' this get around, how you sold out this range to sheep! And, by God, I'll beat the truth out of Mankey! Maybe I'll be back in a day or so with a murder warrant to serve on you! From now on, I'm not ownin' up to the fact that the same women mothered us!"

His jaw was thrust out, and his expression was one of righteous indignation and helpless anger. Abruptly he turned around and strode to the door, throwing it open as Bill stepped aside, saying: "Let's get out of here, Brand. The air's so damn' foul I'm chokin'!"

Outside on the street once more, the lawman let his breath out in a long, relieved sigh. "That done some good, I reckon, just gettin' it off my chest."

"You said plenty," Bill agreed.

They started back toward the jail office. When they had gone a few strides, Ben said: "Things are goin' to start happenin' around here, Brand. I've got a line on this business, and I'll follow it down if it costs me every vote at the next election. But it's nothin' for you to buy into. You'd better be leavin' today, now. Bostwick's crew are after your scalp. If you get into any trouble, it's bound to come out who you are."

"Say the word and I'll stick around and help," Bill said.

Ben shook his head, and once more his face had assumed that familiar gentleness of expression that was reflected in his eyes. "I'll handle Mankey. You and me are about square on this. I had a hunch I could trust you with a job. You done it better'n any man I could have hired. And you've got my thanks. Take that black gelding of Ray's and head north into Utah, like I said the other night. You've got my word for it that another week will see Tom Bostwick back at his lay-out. I'll bust the charge wide open!"

Bill was frowning thoughtfully. He said: "There's a little something I'd like to take care of before I leave. It won't take long." He slowed his stride, and turned toward the edge of the walk.

Ben asked: "Somethin' you'd care to tell me about, Brand?"

"I reckon not."

Bill went out across the dirty street and along it to the hotel. Ben stood watching him, curious, mildly worried. In the end his curiosity got the better of him. He crossed the street and climbed the steps to the wide hotel verandah. Inside, in the lobby, he glanced around and saw that the only occupant was Henry Adler, the clerk, who sat with his feet cocked up on his desk, reading a paper.

"Seen that deputy of mine, Hank?" the sheriff asked, leaning on the counter.

The clerk jerked his head toward the stairway. "He come in a minute ago."

"How long's he goin' to be here?"

Adler shrugged. "I wouldn't know. He asked me the number to Ann Bostwick's room."

"Thanks. I'll wait outside," Ben said, keeping his tone to a casual level. Inwardly he was wondering what business Bill Duncan could possibly have with Tom Bostwick's girl. On his way back to the office, he began looking on things suspiciously, remembering small details. In the end he couldn't be sure that Bill Duncan's memory was as poor as it seemed. For in these last two days he had unknowingly furnished Bill with every clue to his past. He'd been so certain that Bill couldn't remember that he'd given him a fairly true story of what had happened at Halfway Springs, given it to him to use against Tom Bostwick. Bill had seen the money belt. Bill knew about Ray Mankey, or at least part of Mankey's doings. Thinking back over these past twenty minutes, Ben saw his conversation with his brother as being very unconvincing.

The more he thought about it, the more panicky he became. Had Bill Duncan known the truth all along and pretended this loss of memory? Was Duncan up there with Ann Bostwick now, telling her what had happened, how he'd put the blinders on the sheriff and let him go ahead with things that would mean the hang noose in the end if they were known?

Ben Alcott wasn't sure of a thing now. He stood at his office window, nervously mulling his problem over and over again in his mind, and, as he tried to think it all out, he was watching the hotel steps.

As Bill knocked at the door to Room 8 on the second floor of the hotel, he was wishing he hadn't given way to the impulse that had sent him up here. He wouldn't be welcome, and now he wondered what he could say to explain what was on his mind. He heard Ann Bostwick's light tread crossing the room. Then the door swung open, and he was facing her, not knowing how to begin.

She had been smiling as she opened the door. The smile disappeared instantly as she recognized him. Bill could see her head tilt up defiantly, and, when she spoke, her voice held a reserved cool tone: "What do you want?"

He took off his Stetson and fingered its wide brim

anxiously. At length, he said haltingly: "I . . . I'm leavin' town, miss. I wanted to speak to you first."

"Have we anything to talk about?" she asked.

"I don't reckon you have. But I do. I wanted you to know I'm sorry for what happened."

She laughed softly, a laugh that lacked any sign of amusement. "You should have thought of that two days ago . . . if you really mean it."

"I do," he said at once, then added: "We, me and the sheriff, have been over at the bank. Something's come up you should know about. The sheriff's going to help all he can."

"I can imagine Ben Alcott helping us," she said sarcastically. She waited a moment, then asked in irritation: "Well, what is it?"

"They drove sheep onto your graze this mornin'. I saw it happen. When Ben heard about it, he blew up. Both of us have been goin' at this thing wrong, I reckon. He knows it now, and he'll see that it's made up to you."

"How?" Her tone was caustic, bitter, and a hint of tears came to her eyes. "How can it? The law says we've lost the place. He can't fight the law. He *is* the law."

"But he'll see that things are made right," Bill insisted. "I heard him say he would."

"If he said that, he lied! The day's long past when Ben Alcott would do Tom Bostwick a favor." Her manner was defiant, scornful. She was beautiful now, and a dull wave of strange longing swept Bill, a longing for a normal life instead of the outcast's, a longing for the right to call a girl like Ann Bostwick his friend.

"The sheriff went to the bank to see his brother. I was with him. John Alcott won't soon forget the tongue-lashin' Ben gave him."

"Talk has always been one of Ben Alcott's strong points," Ann said bitterly. She seemed all at once aware of standing here and talking to the man who had succeeded in arresting her father where the sheriff had failed. A strong loathing edged into her glance. She said proudly: "I hope you realize what you've done!" The door started swinging shut. "I hope you'll always remember and be ashamed! I . . . I never want to see you again!"

He had a last glimpse of her, biting her lower lip, choking back a sob. Then the door closed, and he stood there, hat in hand, numbed with self-loathing and that impotent feeling of wanting to help Ann Bostwick and not knowing how to do it.

His steps dragged as he walked back along the hallway and down the stairs. He went down the street and crossed to the jail with the feeling of having lost something back there that was vital to him and not knowing what it was.

He climbed wearily into the saddle of the black, remembering once more the debt of gratitude he owed Rawhide's lawman. He glanced across the walk to the jail office window and saw Ben Alcott, standing there. He would have liked to go in and have a last word with the sheriff, but all he wanted was to leave this place as quickly as he could, to be alone and put a shameful part of his past behind him. So he pretended not to see Alcott and reined the black out into the street and headed along it, taking the trail he'd followed the other night, the one that led toward Wagon Fork and across the hills to the north.

VIII

Ben Alcott came out of his office before Bill had turned out of the far end of the street. The lawman's steps were hurried as he crossed the street and pushed open the swing doors to the Peacock.

Inside, he saw Slim and Red and the third Wagon Fork crewman bellied up to the bar. The flush on Slim's face told him that the tall man was well started on one of his periodical drunks. That pleased him, for, drunk, Slim could be a mean and dangerous man.

Without going on in through the doors, he called: "Slim, you and Red busy?" When Slim turned, he nodded back over his shoulder and said: "See you across the way."

Before they could answer, he turned and went back along the walk.

Less than a minute later they were opening the screen door to his office. He was sitting at his desk, and, as they came in, he ignored their suspicious glances and nodded to a pair of chairs ranged along the side wall near the jail door.

Slim glanced at the gun rack above the desk where his gun belt, along with those of the rest of Bostwick's crew, hung. He said dryly: "Thanks. We'll stand!" His attitude was plainly antagonistic, as was Red's, who stood spraddle-legged in the doorway. Both of them were remembering that at two o'clock this morning they'd been put under a peace bond, that the sheriff had kept their guns.

Ben decided to come at once to the point. He said: "I've got it pretty straight that about four thousand head of sheep were driven onto your graze this mornin'."

"You don't say," Slim said with sarcasm. "And, of course, you didn't know anything about it."

Ben ignored the jibe. "I've also got it pretty straight that this new deputy of mine, Pete Brand, was in on the sheep deal. Believe it or not, I wasn't."

Slim's expression changed subtly. At the mention of the new deputy, he seemed to forget his belligerence toward the sheriff. He said: "Nothin' that jasper did would surprise me."

"The worst part is," Ben went on, playing up Slim's interest in Bill, "that not ten minutes ago I paid him off and let him ride out of here. He was mighty anxious to get out for some reason. Too anxious, I thought. So I started thinkin' back. Here's what I remembered."

He tilted back in his chair and reached down to pull open one of the drawers of his desk. He took out the crumpled Reward dodger he'd three nights ago shown

Bill Duncan and held it out to Slim. Slim came across and took it and looked at it. Then, with a glance back over his shoulder, he handed it to Red, saying grimly: "Have a look at this."

Red inspected the printed notice. Ben didn't wait for his comment but said: "Now that I've found this, several things that've happened add up to make sense. You've thought all along I was against Bostwick, playin' along with the bank to sell out the Wagon Fork. It hasn't been me. It's been this Pete Brand!"

He paused, and in that interval both Slim's and Red's glances clung to him eagerly, hanging onto his words. He went on: "First, there was the killing of that sheepherder. I blamed your bunch for that, and, when the big augur of that sheep outfit swore out the warrant, I tried to serve it. I bogged down there. On the way back from your lay-out, I ran into this Pete Brand, found him stranded out there in the desert with his scalp split open. I brought him in and got Doc Robbins to work on him."

"We heard about that," Slim put in.

Ben nodded. "Now figure it this way," he said. "Supposin' this Pete Brand had been here all along. Supposin' he was the one who was hired to cut down that sheepherder and start all this trouble. And say he and another gent followed me to Wagon Fork the day I tried to arrest Bostwick and saw me headin' back without Bostwick. I came across the Bottleneck that day to save some time. I was in a hurry, but I didn't wear out my jughead. They could have. . . ."

"They could've circled on ahead and fixed it so Brand would meet you," Slim interrupted.

"Now you've got it," Ben said. He leaned forward in his chair, pointed at Slim, and wagged his finger to emphasize his point. "Doc Robbins says a bullet cut open Brand's scalp. I say it was a gun barrel. He had whoever was with him slug him over the head with his iron on purpose and leave him there to meet me. Chances are that the gent who sided him was watchin' what happened from less than a quarter mile away."

"That could be," Red agreed.

"All right." Ben tilted back once more in his chair. "You haven't heard what happened that first night after Robbins finished fixin' up Brand's head. Brand claimed he was broke and out of a job. Asked me if I knew of any work. He looked salty, and he wore his iron like he knew how to use it. Your bunch had rawhided me off the place that afternoon, and I was sore."

"So you offered to pay him if he'd bring Bostwick in?" Red asked.

The sheriff tilted his head in the affirmative. "I did. And when Bostwick broke out of jail two nights ago, Brand had an idea how to take him again and at the same time make that eviction notice stick. It was his idea to get out there ahead of time and take your bunch by surprise, before you were ready. It worked."

"I'll say it worked," Slim put in dryly.

"Last night I left Brand out there to watch the place. This mornin', so I hear, there's four thousand head of sheep spread over that mesa pasture. How could they have gotten there unless Brand rode to the sheep camp and told them everything was clear?"

Slim and Red were silent, cold sober, and for the space of a full quarter minute no one spoke. It was Slim who finally said: "Why unload your worries to us? You got yourself in this spot. Get out of it!"

Ben lifted his hands in a helpless gesture. "I'm tied down here with a prisoner to watch. I'm played out from two nights without sleep. Mankey's out there at Bostwick's place, probably raisin' hell and doin' what he can to keep the stinkin' critters from foulin' the yard and corrals. I nccd your help."

Slim nodded toward the gun rack over the desk, saying tartly: "That's a laugh!"

There was a shrewd light in Ben Alcott's eyes now. He got up from the chair and took Slim's double belts down, then Red's single holster. "Have 'em back here by dark," he said.

Belting his gun on, Slim asked: "Which way did Brand head out?"

"North."

"That notice says dead or alive, don't it?" Red queried.

The lawman nodded. "Says he's dangerous when armed, too. Don't take any chances."

IX

A hot wind, blowing in off the desert, followed him, lifting the trail dust kicked up by the black and laying it around Bill in a thin and penetrating fog. He pulled his bandanna up to his squinted eyes and rode with head tilted downward against the reflected sun glare. He didn't hurry, for what lay ahead, his future, seemed empty and uninviting and didn't matter. The thing that mattered was what he was leaving behind him, trouble he had helped build, trouble dragging down people he had learned to respect.

Common sense told him that Ben Alcott would see the Bostwicks through their trouble. But even this small consolation deserted him when he realized that the sheriff was only one man fighting his brother's money and the obviously powerful influence of the sheep interests. He would have turned back then but for the knowledge that he, an outlaw, could do little to help Tom Bostwick and Ann. He had played his hand out, and there was nothing more he could do. If he stayed, his name and reputation would be known in the end, and all Ben Alcott's good intentions on making a reformed man of him would be in vain. No, there was no turning back now.

Four miles from Rawhide he came to the branching in the trails and took the one leading directly north to a high area between the far peaks. Wagon Fork's trail struck off obliquely to the left to skirt the end of the

Bottleneck and climb gradually to the high mesa in the foothills. He glanced along that trail, thinking bitterly that, if fate hadn't twice sent him along it, Tom Bostwick wouldn't be in jail now and Ann wouldn't be living out of a trunk in a hotel room facing a future as blank as his own.

Presently the trail descended and took him into a belt of gaunt and rocky country below the green foothills, a narrow badlands offshoot of the desert. Down here he was out of the wind, but there was a new discomfort to replace the old. The vast reaches of sand and rock and the many uptilted ledges of outcroppings caught and reflected the sun's glare in a nest as fierce as that around a blacksmith's forge. His throat went dry, and his eyes smarted against the blinding glare. He went doggedly on, putting his attention only to keeping the black on the twisting trail.

He was riding that way, loosely, unwarily, when he happened to raise his glance to scan the promise of the green foothills, upward and beyond. It was this glance that showed him, barely seventy yards ahead, the two riders who sat their horses, flanking the line of the trail.

He immediately recognized the flour-sacking sling that cradled Slim's right arm and the flat-crowned Montana Stetson that marked Red Short. He hesitated a bare fraction of a second, coming erect in the saddle and tightening his hold on the reins, then, with the conviction that he couldn't outride whatever threat they offered, he let the black go on.

When he was within twenty feet of them, he reined the black to a stand, seeing that Slim held the reins in his bad hand, that his left was hidden, and noticing Red's unfriendly maneuver of pushing his roan horse to the opposite side of the trail so that they had him between them.

For a full ten seconds none of them spoke. Slim's thin face was set in its habitual reserve. Red, less careful, made his hostility plain by the down-lipped scowl on his ruddy face.

It was Slim who finally spoke, saying flatly: "You left without sayin' your good byes, Brand."

Bill looked steadily from one to the other but made no reply, a coolness running along his nerves at Slim's words that were a clear warning.

Red said: "Yeah, we didn't get our chance to see you off. So we come all this way to make up for it."

Again a silence fell between them. During that interval Bill noticed that they were carrying their guns. That puzzled him, for he'd seen those weapons hanging from the gun rack in the sheriff's office only an hour ago.

It should have warned him of what was coming, but it didn't. Slim's good hand lifted into sight lazily. It was fisting a short-barreled .45 Colt. The gun fell squarely into line with Bill as the thin man drawled: "I've laid Red a bet that you'd fall apart without that gun to back your guts. Shed it and let's see!"

Red swung down out of his saddle on the heel of Slim's words. Bill made no move as the sorrel-topped 'puncher threw his Stetson aside, unbuckled his gun, and laid it on the hat, and then started rolling up his sleeves. He was a big man, not overly tall but heavy-framed and without an ounce of fat to him.

"Maybe you don't hear good," Slim insisted, as Bill made no move. "I said to shed the hardware!"

Bill gave him a level look, slow anger rising in him. It didn't make sense for Slim and Red to be here, and it didn't make sense for them to be carrying guns. He said: "Who sent you?"

"Who cares who sent us?" Red said. "Climb down, Brand. I'm goin' to take you apart!"

Bill thought then that he knew the answer to the part these two were playing in this maze of intrigue. His hands moved to the buckle of his gun belt. He was careful as he uncinched it and hung it from the horn of his saddle. Then, swinging aground, he said: "So you two sided John Alcott on the sheep deal?"

He saw the utter surprise that came into their expressions and knew he was wrong. Slim said in biting sarcasm: "Yeah, we sold out Bostwick. We're out here after another easy haul. Me and Red are going to split the reward on you."

Bill had stepped out from his horse so that now he stood within eight feet of Red. Slim's words stopped him in his tracks. He shot a look at the tall man, knowing suddenly that Ben Alcott was the only man who could have sent them out here. That realization filled him with alarm, knocking the props out from under all his reasoning of these past two days.

He said warily: "What else did Ben Alcott tell you?"

Slim's mirthless smile told him his guess had been a shrewd one. The tall man glanced around, at the twenty-foot stretch of sandy level ground that ran out on all sides, at the sheer high face of a rock outcropping a few feet behind Red, at the dead and stunted growth of a gray-limbed cedar a few feet to Bill's left. He seemed to approve of the spot they had picked.

All at once Slim looked at Red, nodded, and said: "Let him have it!"

Instantly, to Bill's right, Red's boots slurred in the sand. As Bill whipped his glance back to the Wagon Fork man, he instinctively stepped aside and ducked. Red's two leaping steps had already covered the distance between them. He swung both fists in his sudden rush. His left arced through empty air, throwing him slightly off balance so that his hard right slid off Bill's hunched shoulder as he drove on past.

As Bill came up out of his crouch, jabbing hard with left and right at Red's exposed side, he soberly realized the terrific strength of the man he faced. Three inches more of reach and forty pounds of weight were odds that Bill instinctively respected. As his blows drove the breath soughing out of Red's lungs, he wheeled around and took a backward step. Red whirled and crouched, grinning now and saying smoothly: "Not bad for a runt."

Slim called: "Careful, Red! He's fast!"

Red's grin broadened. He lunged one step, stopped suddenly, straightened, and feinted with his right.

Bill rolled out of the way. Red's left caught him as he moved, caught him hard on one cheek in a drive that prolonged his roll to a sprawl. He went to hands and knees, shaking his head to clear it, and then crawled quickly out of the way of Red's kicking boot.

Springing to his feet, Bill sensed that this was to be a tooth-and-nail brawl, nothing barred. From deep within him rose a fierce but cool excitement, some long-forgotten instinct for this kind of a fight. This time he was the one who moved in, arms crossed before his face, head hunched between his shoulders. Red struck him hard in the chest. He came on, stepped inside the next blow, and then brought his knee up hard. It buried itself in Red's mid-section. Red groaned, throwing his arms around Bill's shoulders in a vise-like grip. Bill jerked his hand up, catching Red under the chin. The big man's teeth clicked audibly; his hold slacked off. Bill twisted his shoulders free, backed away, and threw a left and a right to Red's head. His right connected with Red's left ear, his left with the point of the big man's jaw. Red went down, falling forward and with arms outstretched in a vain effort to reach Bill.

Bill let him fall, drawing breath deeply into lungs that were still constricted from the force of that crushing punch of a moment ago. He moved to one side as Red came to his feet again. Red's mouth was bleeding, and a thin line of crimson came down from one corner of his full lips to his jutting chin. But he was clear-headed and a fierce light of hatred surface-glinted his eyes as he came erect.

Bill could see the workings of Red's mind, the sudden resolution to fight cautiously. Before he had planned how to meet these new tactics, Red was coming at him again, slowly this time, head and guard up, moving on his toes.

Bill jabbed out twice with his left, opening his guard and inviting Red to strike. Red's fists moved in tight arcs to flick aside those jabs. He kept coming on. Bill ducked and wove to one side, but still Red refused to be tricked off his guard. Bill retreated two steps. He felt, rather than saw, the closeness of the sheer face of the high outcropping at his back and knew that he could retreat no farther. He suddenly moved to one side, but Red moved with him. The big man's intent was plain now. He wanted to back Bill close in to the outcropping, so that he couldn't move out of the way, and then trust to brute strength to end the fight.

For an instant Bill was panicked, seeing that he fought a cool head now. That must have showed in his eyes, for all at once Red closed in. He threw out his left in a wide sweep that beat aside Bill's guard. His right streaked in. Bill saw the blow coming and tried to dodge backward. But half a step brought him solidly with his back to the rock wall. Then Red's rock-hard knuckles were crushing into his right ear.

His head snapped back. A sharp cutting edge of the outcropping bit into his scalp above his left temple on the tender healing flesh of the bullet-wound. He felt the rock grind through yielding flesh and strike the bone. Blinding pain hit him in an engulfing wave. A nausea clutched him at the pit of his stomach. Retching, his knees went loose, and it was only instinct that made him raise his arms to shield his face as he pushed outward in a rolling fall. He struck the ground hard on his right shoulder. The lance of pain in his head made him lie inert.

Red's boot striking him in the side of his chest emptied his lungs in a convulsive surge. He barely noticed that, for in this last second a myriad of confused thoughts and images had begun racing through his consciousness. He saw the camp at Halfway Springs, the water hole, his saddle, and the money belt. He felt the blow of the rifle bullet alongside his head. He remembered what followed, the long night's aimless walk across the desert reaches, the meeting with Ben Alcott the next afternoon. He remembered Tom Bostwick, Ann, John Alcott, Ray Mankey. He suddenly knew who he was—Bill Duncan, and not Pete Brand.

The pain in his head had dulled now. He found that he could breathe. He opened his eyes and saw Red, standing spraddle-legged above him. He said in a calm voice: "Lay off, Red. I'm whipped."

"Like hell!" Red growled, his face twisted savagely in pure hatred.

The big man swung his boot in another kick. Bill rolled away from it. Then, reaching out, he caught Red's boot and twisted it with what was left of his strength. He caught the surprised expression that crossed Red's battered face. Then Red was staggering off balance and going down onto his knees.

They came up together. Bill's senses were steady now, and his breath had surged into his lungs in a gust that seemed to give him new strength. He didn't wait this time, didn't plan out a way of tackling Red. He rushed in on the big man with a suddenness that caught Red by surprise. Red's arms came up to shield his face. Bill threw all his weight into his shoulders and drove both fists in at the man's broad chest. Red's hands instinctively came down to protect his wind. Bill hit him in the face with a hard right. Then, stepping back to gather all his weight behind his left, he arced it in a blow that began at the level of his knees and ended on the sorrel-thatched 'puncher's jutting chin.

The impact of bone on bone was clearly audible. A burning pain coursed up along the back of Bill's left hand and into his wrist. He knew that he had broken a bone. But Red's eyes had gone glassy. With that signal, Bill waded in again. He threw a right, a left, and a harder right, and Red's head rocked with the blows. Red's knee joints failed him, and he fell into Bill. Bill caught him, tried to stand him erect again, and then they both fell, Red rolling to one side.

Bill pushed himself up onto his feet and stood on shaking legs, breathing hard, looking down at Red who hadn't moved a muscle.

From off to his right, Slim's voice taunted: "There's still this, Brand!"

Bill had forgotten Slim. He looked across and saw

him hunched over the saddle, his good arm resting on the horn and holding the gun leveled squarely.

He started across toward Slim.

The tall man straightened. "Stay back, Brand!"

But Bill came on until Slim's thumb drew back the hammer of the weapon. He stooped then, within two or three paces of the pony's head, and said: "Slim, I'm not Brand. I'm Bill Duncan." His hand came up to the gash on his scalp and ran along his sticky wet hair. He brought the hand away, holding it palm out so that the tall man could see the smear of blood. "When Red knocked my head back against that rock, it brought it all back. I can remember now."

Slim's gaunt face shaped a mirthless grin. "You've sure got a slick tongue, Brand."

Bill crowded back his irritation before a long-trained patience, saying: "Did you read that letter I wrote Tom Bostwick, the one Bill Duncan wrote?"

Slim moved his head slowly in a negative, the grin not relaxing. "It won't work, Brand."

"I can repeat that letter to you word for word."

"Don't bother. I didn't see it. Neither did you."

"I can tell you who my father was, the year he came here with Bostwick, when he died."

The gun in Slim's hand didn't waver. He drawled: "You could've picked all that up talkin' to Ben Alcott. Besides, I don't know a thing about the Duncans." He wasn't giving an inch.

Bill squatted on his heels there, two paces from the bay pony's head. He looked levelly at Slim, saying:

"You're a jughead! I'm Duncan. I've got enough on Ben Alcott to hang him, if you'll help."

"Ben's all right. Me and the rest have had him figured wrong all along. He was meanin' to help. You're the one that brought on all this trouble, and Ben was just a little slow gettin' wise to you."

"Ben and his brother framed Bostwick. I've even seen that money belt of mine with the five thousand in it in Ben's safe." Bill picked up a handful of sand and let it sift between his fingers.

Slim laughed softly, mockingly: "This is fun, seein' you try and beg your way loose. As soon as I bring Red around, we'll be goin'."

"You're takin' me in?"

"Dead or alive," Slim assured, hefting his weapon to emphasize his words. "And I sure as hell can use my half of the reward."

Bill's hand came up slowly, fisting another handful of sand. Suddenly his arm whipped back, and he threw the sand straight at the pony's head, lunging sideways. The pony shied, reared on hind legs, and Slim's gun exploded in a burst of sound that racketed out against the stillness. His bullet kicked at the exact spot Bill's boots had left a split second ago. Bill had thrown himself up at Slim in a headlong dive.

He hit Slim, shoulder first. Slim lost his balance, the horse wheeled, and they both rolled from the saddle. As he fell, Bill wrapped his arms around Slim. His left hand whipped out to strike Slim on the wrist and knock his gun from his hand.

The pony wheeled away as they fell, throwing Slim underneath. His body took up the impact as they hit the ground, driving the wind from his lungs and stunning him momentarily as his head whipped back and hit the ground. Bill hit Slim on the temple, not hard, but in a blow that loosened every muscle of the thin man's long frame.

Bill pushed himself erect, took Slim's guns, and rammed them through the waist band of his Levi's. Then he went across to pick up his Stetson and his own weapon and belt and cinched it on. He looked across at Red, who hadn't moved. He stood in thought a moment, then reached into his pocket, and brought out a clasp knife.

In the next two minutes he caught up the roan and the bay and cut the cinches on Slim's and Red's saddles. Then he walked over to vault into the black's saddle, wheeling the animal around as he let a last, inspecting glance go to the two fallen Wagon Fork men. Red was still lying inertly. Slim had moved his legs, and, as Bill watched, he made a vain effort to sit up but couldn't get his arms to support his weight.

Bill reined over to the trail and started back along it toward Rawhide, the black at a reaching run.

X

Rawhide's single street was nearly empty under the blaze of the mid-afternoon sun as Bill rode the black into its far limits. A dozen fly-worried saddle horses and buckboard teams stood at the tie rails before the awninged walks fronting the stores at the town's center. Occasionally a man could be seen moving lazily along the walks, but aside from these signs of life the town seemed listless under the scorching heat. The walk and the hitch rail before the jail were deserted.

Bill reined the black to the near side of the street a hundred yards short of the jail. He rode in under the generous shade of a big cottonwood and came out of the saddle there, tying his horse to a limb of the tree and taking to the dirt walk. Going along it, he was wondering how to use the surprise Ben Alcott was sure to feel at seeing him.

He came to the plank walk a few yards short of the jail but made no attempt to walk carefully. He hesitated a brief instant short of the jail office window, then in one long stride stepped past it and wheeled into the office doorway, right hand closed about the handle of his Colt.

The office was empty. Ben Alcott's swivel chair was turned away from the desk. In the ashtray on the desk the three-inch stub of a cigar smoldered, sending a thin finger of blue smoke curling lazily upward. That sign of recent occupancy tuned Bill to a high-pitched wariness. The insistent low *buzzing* of a fly against the screen was the only sound that broke the stillness. His glance went back to the jail door. That reassured him, for the door was propped shut by the top rung of a chair's back wedged against the bottom of the broken lock. Ben Alcott couldn't be in his jail.

He stepped back into the doorway and took one last look along the street. Not a man moved on the walks. Dropping his gun back into leather, he crossed to the back of the office, lifted the chair out of the way, and opened the jail door. The heat and stuffiness of the semi-dark room were more pronounced than he remembered.

Tom Bostwick's heavy frame was stretched out on the cot in the first cell. He turned his head at the sound of the door's opening, saw who it was, and slowly lowered his boots to the floor and sat up. His grizzled face was set in a faintly belligerent look, and his brown-green eyes were unfriendly. A gray beard stubble covered his cheeks and blunt jaw, adding to the severity of his face.

Bill said: "Where's the sheriff?"

Tom Bostwick let a moment's silence run out before he answered: "Went out a few minutes ago with a woman. She claimed her husband was drunk, and she wanted him jailed until he sobered up. Ben went after him."

Bill took tobacco and papers from his pocket and came across the narrow corridor to lean against the bars at the front of the cell. He began building a smoke, looking down at his hands, and finally said in a quiet voice: "My old man said something before he died maybe you'd like to know about, Bostwick. It went something like this. 'If you're ever in real trouble and need help, go to Tom Bostwick. He's worth any three friends I ever had.' I've remembered that. I'm in trouble now, so here I am."

He waited, not looking up from the cigarette. He heard the cot frame creak, heard Tom Bostwick step across the cell and close in to him.

He went on: "In case that don't settle it, you came out here with Dad in Eighteen Sixty-Nine and started the Wagon Fork as partners. He left you to head on west in the early spring of Eighteen Seventy-Four, the year you were married. He took three men of the crew, old Sid Remington and Bill Larus and Shorty Smith, along with three hundred head of prime three-year-olds. On the way, he stopped at Fort Yuma for three weeks, long enough to court and marry my mother, Sarah, who was Colonel Singleton's daughter. She went on with him, and after another month's drive they made the headwaters of Catamount Creek. Dad threw up a shack there, and he and his three men homesteaded along the creek. I was born two years later and. . . ."

His words broke off as Tom Bostwick's hand shot out through the bars and clamped his arm in a vise-like grip. Bostwick's hoarse voice grated: "How the hell do you know all this?"

Bill raised his glance and met the wide-open stare of the rancher's eyes. He said: "I'm Bill Duncan, Bost-wick."

Disbelief and ready anger came to the rancher's eyes. Suddenly his hand dipped and snatched the nearest of Slim's guns from the waist band of Bill's

Levi's. He backed away, leveling the weapon and saying harshly: "Now, by God, talk and talk straight!"

Bill took off his Stetson, turning his head so that Bostwick could see the blood-matted hair along his scalp. "Remember that first day, Bostwick?" he asked. "My head was bandaged. It was bandaged because Ben Alcott the day before found me strayin' around out in the desert without a horse and with no hat and with my head cut open. I keeled over tryin' to shoot Ben, on the crazy idea that he was the man who'd bushwhacked me the night before at my camp at Halfway Springs. He brought me in, had the doctor work on me. When I came to, I couldn't remember anything that had happened. When Ben made sure of that, he told me I was this outlaw, Pete Brand, and sicced me onto a job he couldn't do himself, bringin' you in to jail."

The gun in Tom Bostwick's hand wavered and sagged at Bostwick's side. Bill went on: "Ben used me until today, when I happened to find out that sheep were bein' driven onto your place. After that, this mornin', he got rid of me as quick as he could. I was headed out of here for Utah. Ben got Slim and Red, gave them their guns, and sent them out after me, tellin' them they could have the reward on me if they brought me in. They caught up with me. I tangled with Red and got my head banged again. It was a hard enough jolt so that it brought me to. I remembered everything. So here I am."

"You *are* Bill Duncan," the rancher breathed. It was a statement of fact and no longer a question.

Bill nodded.

After a moment, the strained expression left Bostwick's grizzled face, and he was smiling broadly. "I thought I was losin' my wits," he said. "That first day I claimed you looked like your old man. You do. When it turned out you were someone else, I began doubtin' my eyes. They didn't fool me, after all. You. . . ."

The sudden upswing of Bill's hand motioned him to silence. Bill turned, and from the office came the banging of the street's screen door. Bill palmed one of Slim's guns from the belt of his pants and took two soundless, quick strides that put him behind the jail door.

He was barely out of sight when Ray Mankey strode into the jail from the office. The deputy's glance went along the corridor and then to Bostwick's cell, suspicion flaring alive in his eyes. He snapped out: "What's this door doin' open? Where's Ben?"

Behind him, Bill drawled: "Mankey."

Ray Mankey spun around. At sight of the gun in Bill's fist, his hand strayed two inches closer to the holster at his right thigh, then froze. Slowly he raised both hands, saying flatly: "What the hell is this?"

"Got your keys, Ray?" Bill asked.

Mankey nodded.

"Throw 'em over here."

Mankey didn't move. Finally he said: "Not until you tell me why you want 'em."

"To let Bostwick out."

Mankey's thick-featured face went ugly. Bill took a step toward him, another, a quicker one, to the side. His gun swung up in a tight arc as he stepped in toward Mankey. The deputy struck out blindly with one hand, ducking aside. He wasn't quick enough. The barrel of the Colt crushed in the crown on his pearl-gray Stetson. Mankey's breath soughed out of his lungs in a prolonged groan. His knees went loose, and he fell forward into Bill's arms.

Bill stretched him out face up on the floor. His hand went to one of Mankey's pockets and came out holding a ring of keys. He thrust the gun he had taken from Slim back behind his belt, and then turned to the cell door. In fifteen more seconds Tom Bostwick was stepping out of the cell.

Bostwick said: "Now what?"

"We're goin' to open that safe. My money, that five thousand, is in there. The way it got there is that Mankey must've been the man that shot me at Halfway Springs."

Leading the way through the door to the office, Tom Bostwick said flatly: "They had it planned all along, stoppin' you on your way here, foreclosing on the lay-out, and selling it over to sheep. Bill, I've got some accounts to settle today."

"You mean *we* have," Bill said, stepping around the rancher to the safe beside the desk at the back wall. He eyed it a moment, saying finally: "If we could bring Mankey around, we'd make him open it for us."

Bostwick shook his head. "Ray's got mulish guts. He wouldn't do it."

"Then we'll try this." Bill drew the .45 from his holster and lined it at the round dial of the combination, thumbing back the hammer. As an afterthought, he said: "Better take a look down the street, Tom."

Bostwick went to the door, pushed back the screen, and in a moment called: "Go ahead!"

The concussion of the deafening explosion rattled the window. Bostwick turned from the door to see Bill squatting before the safe and pulling the door open. The nickeled combination dial was smashed. Then Bill was facing around, holding out a webbed money belt with bulging pouches. He shook it so that the clink of gold coins sounded clearly.

He said: "The first thing ought to be to go see John Alcott. Maybe he'll extend your time limit on the loan a day!"

Bostwick's beard-stubbled face broke into a broad smile. "Not a bad idea." Then he frowned, nodding out onto the street. "What'll we say about that shot?"

"Don't say anything. No one's goin' to try stoppin' us."

Bill took the money belt in one hand, his gun in the other, and crossed the room and went out onto the walk, Bostwick close behind. They started down the walk. Across the street a man was running toward them. When he saw them, he stopped, his eyes opened wide in astonishment, and he called back over his shoulder to a second man standing in a nearby doorway. What he said was unintelligible.

Beneath the wooden awning that shaded the walk thirty yards ahead stood a group of three men who were looking up toward the jail. Their glances reflected the same astonishment as the man's across the street when they saw Bill and Tom Bostwick approaching. They backed to the edge of the walk as Bill and the rancher came closer. Striding past them, Tom Bostwick spoke to one, a man Bill recognized as a Wagon Fork man.

"Larry, get an iron and keep the crowd off our backs while we're in the bank!"

Bill said—"Here, Larry."—and handed the 'puncher his gun. He drew Slim's second gun from his belt, and Larry fell in behind them as they went on, not saying a word. They strode on that way, Bill and the rancher in the lead, Larry two paces behind. The walk had been deserted a minute ago. Now, miraculously, men appeared in nearly every store doorway and on the walk itself. Across the street it was the same. Half a hundred pair of eyes followed the progress of that trio under the wide awning.

Once Larry said sharply—"Back, Len!"—as a man made a move to step down onto the walk from a doorway they were passing. The man stepped back quickly and stayed in the doorway.

They came out from under the last stretch of wooden awning and into the sun glare, abreast the corner of the brick bank. Bill said: "We'd better put our irons away, in case they think it's a hold-up

245

inside." He holstered his weapon, and Tom Bostwick thrust his into a generous pocket of his pants.

Turning in at the bank's door, they stepped aside to let a woman come out. Her eyes widened in alarm as she saw Tom Bostwick. He said politely—"Good afternoon, Laura."—and stepped on past her into the door to follow Bill.

The teller in the second cage along the wide aisle saw them first. Bill told him—"Take it easy and you won't get hurt, mister."—striding past him and down the long counter beyond the cages. Two of the half dozen customers saw Bostwick and recognized him. One's mouth sagged open, the other leaned over and whispered something to a man alongside. But no one made a move to stop them as Bill kicked open the waist-high door at the end of the counter and crossed the narrow space toward the door with the frosted-glass panel lettered PRESIDENT.

Bostwick said from immediately to his rear: "Let me go in first."

Bill stepped aside. Bostwick turned the knob of the door, and pushed it open. He stood there in the door, and Bill heard him say in deep tones: "This is luck, findin' you in, John!"

Then the rancher was going into the office, and Bill followed.

John Alcott was sitting at his desk. His flabby face was a sickly yellow as he eyed Tom Bostwick. His loose frame was cocked forward in his chair, and his two hands were braced palms down on the desk, as though a moment ago he had started to push himself erect and then had thought better of it.

Bostwick reached around and took the money belt from Bill's hand. He tossed it across toward the desk. It lit with a heavy thud, scattering a pile of papers and knocking a shot-filled pen holder to the floor. It slid across and down onto John Alcott's lap as Tom Bostwick said in a smooth and ominous voice: "There's your five thousand, John. It's a day overdue, but that won't matter, will it? By the way, this is my friend, the Bill Duncan I told you about."

The banker gulped, swallowed with difficulty, and stammered out: "Tom, I swear to God I. . . . I didn't know he was. . . ."

Bostwick cut in: "I'll take that note I signed."

Alcott rose slowly up out of the chair. He nodded toward a big safe in the back corner of the office, saying hoarsely: "It's in there."

"Get it!"

The banker stopped and worked the safe's combination. Bill came around the corner of the desk so that he could watch. Alcott's fingers trembled as they spun the nickeled dial. Once he reached back to wipe the perspiration from his hand on the seat of his pants. He went to work again. Presently the heavy door swung open, and Alcott reached inside.

Bill had had a momentary glimpse of a gun lying on the middle shelf inside the safe. He took a long step that put him alongside the banker. Then he lifted his boot and thrust it hard and down, so that it caught

Alcott's wrist and held it wedged firmly against the corner of the shelf, within finger spread of the weapon.

As Alcott groaned in pain, Bill reached over and picked up the weapon and stepped back. Alcott whirled and cringed back against the safe. His face was drained of all color, and his eyes were wide in fear. He said in a barely audible whisper: "I . . . I wasn't going to touch it!"

"No," Bill said, "you don't pack the guts it takes, do you, Alcott?"

The sound of the door opening made Bill and Tom Bostwick wheel to face it, weapons lined. Larry stood there. He jerked his hand out toward the front of the bank. "I thought you ought to know that the sheriff just walked into his office."

"Thanks, Larry," Bostwick said in even tones. He turned to look at the banker again, thrusting out a hand and saying sharply: "The note!"

Alcott rummaged in the safe until he found a red manila folder. He took it out with trembling hands, opened it, and sorted through some papers, finally taking out one and handing it to Bostwick.

The rancher examined it, smiled thinly, crumpled it, and laid it in the ornate metal ashtray on the desk. He took a match from the holder on the tray, lit it, and touched it to the piece of paper.

As it flared aflame and burned to a gray ash, Bostwick looked at Alcott and said: "John, a while back there was some talk of me and half a dozen other men buyin' out your interest in the bank. Maybe you're ready to sell now."

For a bare instant, stubborn rebellion was mirrored in John Alcott's eyes. Then that look faded. He said hollowly: "I think it can be arranged."

"Good. You've found this dry climate bad for your health, haven't you, John?"

Alcott nodded weakly, and then Bostwick motioned Bill to follow him out the door.

In the high-ceilinged room outside, they found the clerks grouped near the vault door and the customers gathered at the front of the counter. As they appeared, the hum of subdued conversation died. The half dozen customers backed slowly out to the wall on the far side of the aisle as Bill and the rancher came out the gate at the counter end.

Larry was standing just inside the door up front. He nodded out to the street and said: "Slim and Red pulled in a minute ago. They're headed down here now, with Mankey and the sheriff."

Bostwick nodded and strode on. When he was a step short of the door, Bill reached out and took a hold on his arm, saying: "My turn now, Tom."

The rancher shook his head, pulled his arm free, and went on. Bill came alongside him on the side nearest the jail. They came out onto the walk that way and faced down the street.

Sixty feet away, Ben Alcott thrust out a hand and suddenly broke out of his hurried stride. Ray Mankey, alongside him, stopped abruptly. Slim and Red, coming behind the lawman and his deputy, stepped to one side to look ahead down the walk.

Bostwick called: "Slim, step aside! You, too, Red!"

Even at this distance, Bill caught the puzzled expression that crossed Slim's face. Out of the corner of his eye he saw someone move on the hotel verandah across the street. Glancing over there, he had a glimpse of Ann, standing at the verandah railing. She held one clenched hand to her mouth, and there was fear in her eyes. Bill looked up the walk again.

A three-second silence followed. Slim hesitated, bewildered. Red started out toward the edge of the walk when a sudden, low-spoken command from the sheriff stopped him. Then Ben Alcott was calling ominously: "Bostwick, I've deputized your men to help me take Brand! Get out of the way!"

Bostwick said: "It won't work, Ben. I know this man's Bill Duncan."

It took a bare second for the realization that he had walked into a trap to show on Ben Alcott's mild-looking face. It took on an ugly look of wariness.

Suddenly he wheeled around, his right hand stabbing to his holster and his left taking a hold on Slim's arm. He spun in behind the tall man, rammed his gun in Slim's back, and said sharply: "Get back, Ray!"

Mankey took a backward step. Red, near the edge of the walk, turned slowly. Then his hands edged upward as Alcott swung his gun around on him. Mankey's weapon was out now, ready, lined down the walk at Bill.

Alcott called: "Make a move and you'll lose two good men, Bostwick!" He started breaking away, pulling Slim after him.

Bill's short-coupled body was cocked rigidly. He called suddenly: "Drop, Slim!" He leaped to the side, right hand blurring up his gun. He collided with Tom Bostwick, knocking the rancher to one side. At the same time, he saw Slim's tall frame suddenly fold toward the planking of the walk.

He rocked his gun into line and squeezed the trigger at the exact instant Ben Alcott's Colt stabbed flame. The double explosion laid a bursting sound along the cañon of the street. Bill felt the tug of a bullet along his shirt sleeve at the instant he saw Ben Alcott's spare frame jerked backward. The sheriff stumbled, went to his knees.

At the same time Mankey's gun blazed, its explosion prolonging the louder double concussion. Tom Bostwick's gun sounded alongside. Ray Mankey staggered to one side, stumbled over the step of a store's doorway, and sprawled headlong into it.

Bill saw all that even though his attention was centered on Ben Alcott. The sheriff, kneeling behind Slim's sprawled frame, cast only a single glance at his deputy, then brought his gun swinging into line again with startling quickness. A spot of red showed on his shirt at his left shoulder. His face held a wicked, savage look as he rocked his weapon so that he was looking across his sights at Bill.

The move was so unexpected and swiftly timed that

it caught Bill by surprise. His thumb rocked back the hammer of his Colt at the precise instant of Alcott's shot. A blow struck him low along the ribs on his left side, sending a lancing pain up into his chest. His gun swung out of line, then back again. He squeezed the trigger, instinctively aiming high to send his bullet clear of Slim. The heavy .45 whipped back in his hand, and his thumb brought the hammer to cock again on the down swing. Ben's gun stabbed powder smoke once more. Bill ignored it, shot again . . . and again . . . and again, until the weapon's hammer clicked on an empty shell case.

As the dying echoes of that gun burst faded out along the street, Bill stared through a haze of powder smoke to see Ben Alcott, toppling slowly forward. The lawman fell across Slim's outstretched legs. Slim sat up, and Ben's upper body rolled loosely from across his legs onto the walk.

Slim took one look down at the sheriff, his thin face went pale, and he looked up at Red, murmuring: "Better cover his face. It ain't pretty." He spoke quietly and in awed tones, yet his voice carried clearly along the street, so complete was the stillness.

Bill heard Slim's words dimly, through a hollow ringing in his ears. He sat down abruptly on the walk, surprised to find that his legs wouldn't support him. He was vaguely aware of Tom Bostwick's saying—"Lie there and take it easy, Bill. Here comes Doc Robbins."—and of letting Bostwick ease him down the rest of the way onto the walk. He thought he heard

Ann's voice from far away a moment later. He tried hard to catch what she said. But by then the peaceful languor of unconsciousness was crowding in on him.

Bill heard Doc Robbins's voice as a mere whisper of faraway sound. The doctor was saying: " . . . lost plenty of blood, and there's that broken rib. I'm going to take some stitches there where his scalp's cut open. How'd he get that?"

Then Red Short's voice came out of that haze of semi-consciousness. "While he was givin' me the worst beatin' a man ever took. I reckon the one time I hit him did that."

Bill wanted to open his eyes, but couldn't. His thoughts faded out for a while and then came back suddenly at a stab of pain along the side of his head. He winced as the pain came again. Then he opened his eyes.

Doc Robbins was staring down at him. Beyond Robbins was the papered wall of a strange room. The medico's round face took on a smile. "Hurt, didn't it?" he said. "But it's finished now." He turned, looked back over his shoulder, and said to someone: "You can take charge of him."

A light step sounded across the floor near by. Then Ann Bostwick's oval face was looking down at Bill. Robbins got up off the edge of the bed, and Ann sat down where he had been. Her eyes were moist with tears, but there was gladness in them.

She didn't speak for a long moment, until a door

closing softly across the room broke the stillness. Then she said in a low, halting voice: "I . . . I was afraid for a while, Bill. But it's all right now."

He started to speak. She put an arm lightly across his mouth. "You mustn't talk. Everything's all right. You're here in my room at the hotel. Dad and Slim are across at the bank, keeping back the crowd. They want to lynch John Alcott."

For a long moment she smiled down at him. Her look turned sober then, and she said in a voice that was only a whisper: "We wouldn't be going home again if it wasn't for you, Bill. Do you know what you mean to us?"

Bill wanted to ask her if she knew what she meant to him, but her hand across his mouth stopped him.

All at once she took her hand away and leaned down and put her lips where the hand had been. It didn't matter then that he hadn't told her.

Additional Copyright Material

Center Point Publishing
600 Brooks Road ● PO Box 1
Thorndike ME 04986-0001 USA

(207) 568-3717

US & Canada:
1 800 929-9108
www.centerpointlargeprint.com